GETTING
HERS

ALSO BY DONNA HILL

Rhythms

An Ordinary Woman

Rockin' Around That Christmas Tree

In My Bedroom

Divas, Inc.

Anthologies

Rosie's Curl and Weave

Della's House of Style

Going to the Chapel

Sister, Sister

Welcome to Leo's

Let's Get It On

GETTING
HERS

Donna Hill

ST. MARTIN'S PRESS ❊ NEW YORK

www.stmartins.com

Book design by Irene Vallye

Library of Congress Cataloging-in-Publication Data

Hill, Donna (Donna O.)
    Getting hers / Donna Hill.—1st ed.
        p. cm.
    ISBN 0-312-28194-3
    EAN 978-0-312-28194-6
    1. Female friendship—Fiction. 2. Loss (Psychology)—Fiction. 3. Self-realization—Fiction. I. Title.

PS3558.I3864G48 2005
813'.54—dc22

                                                    2004063285

First Edition: June 2005

10 9 8 7 6 5 4 3 2 1

To each and every reader who picked up this book and decided to come along for the ride—thank you! Sit back, relax, and enjoy.

ACKNOWLEDGMENTS

I truly have to thank all of the readers who have been so supportive of my work all these years, in whatever form it takes, and who continue to buy my books and tell their friends! A big shout out of thanks to my editor, Monique Patterson, who has got to be the most patient person in the world! Thanks for putting up with all my drama, Monique. Many thanks to Monica Jackson, Robert, and Michelle for being my sounding boards, listening to me whine, offering great advice, and constantly whispering in my ear, "Girl, you didn't finish that book *yet?*" I cannot thank Monica Harris enough for helping me to refocus on what my story was really about and for getting me back on track. Big thanks and hugs to Ron for providing needed details and for being so easy and understanding. Many thanks to all of my sister and brother authors who remain true to the art while continuing to entertain and inform; Bernice McFadden, Donna Grant and Virginia Deberry, Gwynne Forster, Leslie Esdaile Banks, Vincent Alexandria, Kenji Jasper, Nicole Bailey-Williams, Lolita Files, Victoria Christopher Murray, Kim Roby,

Victor McGlothin, TaRessa, and Francis Ray. I am proud to be among you and to call you friends. There is so much talent out there that the list could go on forever. But none of us could do what we do without blessings from the Higher Power. I thank God for giving me this gift and allowing me to live my dream.

Oh what a tangled web we weave,
when first we practice to deceive.

—Sir Walter Scott

GETTING
HERS

FATE IS A FUNNY THING

"Dearly beloved, we are gathered here today to put to rest the body of our brother, Troy Benning, husband of Kimberly Sheppard-Benning and a friend to many. . . ."

Kim's alabaster complexion was dutifully shielded behind the black veil that dipped down dramatically from her wide-brimmed black hat. She brought a white handkerchief beneath the veil and dabbed at her dry eyes. "Bastard," she muttered.

The reverend droned on about what a wonderful man Troy was while an endless stream of mourners marched up to the grave to toss a rose or utter words of sorrow and condolence to Kim.

Kim scanned the crowd from behind her veil hoping to catch a glimpse of Stephanie. Finally she spotted her, with her arm tucked through that of her husband, Malcolm. Kim's stomach muscles tightened as Stephanie's green-eyed gaze found Kim's blue one. Stephanie offered a slow, sad smile before looking away.

———

On the far side of the proceedings, Tess McDonald desperately
wanted a cigarette. Funerals, cops, predawn phone calls, hot sex,
and situations out of her control always elevated her craving. Ca-
sually, she looked the crowd over. Nothing particularly unusual,
except that someone in attendance murdered Troy Benning.

From the opposite side of the hole, beneath the shadow of a
spanning oak, Nicole Perez murmured "Amen," along with the
others. "And good riddance," she added under her breath.
Nicole clasped her gloved hands together and licked her blood
red lips. From behind dark glasses, her onyx eyes darted around
the throng of mourners, then returned to rest on the hole in the
ground. She swallowed. With all of the situations that she'd
found herself in, even behind bars, she hadn't been afraid—
wary maybe, cautious for sure, but never afraid. She put on a
good front. She had to. No one could ever find out what really
happened. She swallowed hard and tugged in a deep breath.
This would all be over soon and the three of them could move
on with their lives—whatever that might mean.

Two Months Later:
Tess, Nikki, and Kim raised their wineglasses in a quiet toast.

"To us," Tess said, as her lids lowered ever so slightly over
her honey brown eyes and the curve of her wide mouth spread
in a salacious grin, the bold bronze color matching her body-
hugging dress to perfection.

The trio clinked their glasses together as the Amtrak Acela
Express sped out of New York City en route to Washington, D.C.

Expertly coiffed as usual, Kim's signature diamond studs sparkled against the light. Kim lowered her head and her voice to whisper, "I still can't believe it."

"What's not to believe? They tried to fuck us, but we fucked them first," Nicole said with a nonchalant flick of her wrist. Her tennis bracelet flashed. "Ain't that right?" She looked from one woman to the other.

Kim flushed crimson. She spoke from between clenched teeth. "Do you always have to talk like that?" Her blue eyes darted around the dining car to see if anyone in earshot was offended. "We can dress you up but we still can't take you out."

Nicole grinned and gave Kim a wink. "Be careful my little pretty, the wife is always the first suspect."

"Nikki—"

Tess stretched her slender hand across the table and covered Kim's pale fingers with her cocoa brown ones. "Relax. You know Nikki is just being Nikki. She loves to see you flustered, and you fall for it every time."

Kim cut a look in Nicole's direction. Nicole smirked into her glass.

"Philadelphia—Thirtieth Street Station in three minutes," the conductor announced.

Nicole picked up her purse and rose. She looked from one woman to the other and for an instant the bravado vanished from her petite demeanor, and uncertainty flickered in her dark eyes. "Thank you," she said barely above a whisper. She turned and walked away.

"I should be getting back to my car," Kimberly muttered, before polishing off the last of her drink. She stood, cleared her throat and straightened her shoulders as if preparing for a formal speech. "I'm sure we won't be seeing each other again."

A half smile curved Tess's mouth. "You never know," she said slowly.

Kim looked at Tess. Unthinkable questions hung between them. "Take care of yourself, Tess."

"You do the same, Kim." She watched Kim until she was out of sight.

Alone now, Tess leaned back against the blue leather headrest. The rocking motion of the train coupled with the landscape that flashed in the window like small bursts of neon light was almost hynotic. She crossed her legs beneath the table and took a thoughtful sip from her glass of wine.

Over the past few months they'd gone from virtual strangers and wary adversaries to partners in crime—so to speak— revealing and acting upon their deepest secrets, their darkest desires. It had been risky. They'd put their families, their money, themselves in jeopardy. It had taken all of their connections, wits, and determination—but, mostly, it had taken the unholy pact they had made together to get them as far as they'd gotten. She shut her eyes. God, what had she done?

Under normal circumstances they would have never met: she, a black high-priced madam who ran the biggest escort service on the East Coast; Nicole, a Latina beauty with a mouth like a longshoreman and a penchant for guns and fast cars; and Kim, a white, married business tycoon who was in love with the wife of a congressman. But fate, the stars, and the mutual goal of retribution brought them together one blistering afternoon in June. The hottest June day on record . . .

CHAPTER ONE

THE WAITING ROOM

Tess had an old habit of sizing up other women and imagining what their lives must be like. Every now and again, when someone truly struck her fancy, she'd strike up a conversation just to see how close to the mark she was and, ultimately, to determine if the woman had potential for the business. There was a good chance that the women who came to the GYN office were either getting rid of something or making sure that something hadn't gotten them. In other words, they took care of themselves, one of the most important job requirements. Some of her most successful employees had been recruited right here in the waiting room.

Take the white chick, for example, who seemed vaguely familiar to Tess: easy on the eyes, obviously well-off from the cut of her hot pink suit to the diamond studs in her tiny earlobes. Tall, maybe 5'8" or so, aristocratic features, startling blue eyes, and almost too-perfect blond hair. The All-American ideal of beauty. A forty-something businesswoman. Cool and controlled. Some men seemed to enjoy her type—*the ice maiden.* Their goal was to melt down her reserve. Hmmm, a possibility.

The door to the waiting room opened and Tess made a quick appraisal of the sexy Latina that strutted in. Her inky black hair was definitely her calling card—waist length, wavy and lustrous. But her eyes were just as alluring—mesmerizing, Tess noted, when the young woman flashed a short, hot look in her direction. Hmmm. *Passionate.* The petite body was full and ripe as fresh fruit and she obviously didn't mind showing it off, judging by her minimal attire.

Tess made a mental note of the two women who'd drawn her attention. With her business now in shambles and her ladies scattered like windswept leaves, she needed to seriously consider some new recruits if she was going to get back on her feet. Those two definitely had possibility. But she had to be careful.

She picked up a magazine and flipped through the pages.

Kim snapped open her Prada handbag and took out her compact. Checking her reflection, she patted her nose with the cream-colored sponge while studying the woman in white who sat opposite her. Kim caught her staring earlier and briefly wondered if she was "interested." Funny that the thought should even enter her mind. The only woman she'd ever been with since her days of college experimentation was Stephanie Abrams—and definitely not a black woman. She gave a little shiver. She'd heard so many stories about black women and their insatiable sexuality and wondered how much of it was truth or fiction.

It didn't much matter, she concluded, closing her compact and dropping it back into her purse. She had enough to contend with at the moment. She pushed up the sleeve of her Valentino suit, just above her wrist, and checked her platinum Rolex. She certainly hoped the visit wouldn't take long. She was scheduled to meet Stephanie at six. A tingle beat between her thighs at the thought. Kim crossed her stockinged legs and waited.

Nicole took a brief look around and decided on a seat by the window, as far away from everyone as possible.

At least it wasn't crowded, she thought, snatching a quick look at the two women. And the place did have central air, which was a blessing after sleeping in that oven of an apartment.

She stretched out her bare legs and crossed them at the ankle. How much she hated coming to the GYN could not be put into words. The thought of those cold instruments and somebody looking up at her stuff with a light gave her the creeps. Especially now, especially after what she'd been through, which was the main reason why she'd come. Her brother, Ricky, nearly blew a fuse when she told him she was going out.

"I swear, Nikki, if I find out you went anywhere near Trust, I'll put your ass out in the street and you know what your P.O. will do then."

"Chill," she'd snapped, throwing up her palm. "I got a doctor's appointment. The social worker at the joint set it up for me. Okay?" She tossed her hair over her shoulder and planted her hands defiantly on her round hips.

Ricky pressed his lips into a tight line, then pointed a finger of warning in her face. "I mean it."

Nicole rolled her eyes, snatched up her backpack, and walked out, her cut-off denim shorts hugging her plump rear and leaving plenty of room for a good view of her long honey brown legs.

Ever since she came through the door, Ricky had been all over her. She couldn't breathe without him clocking her every breath. As soon as she could pull everything together she was out of there. Good thing this doc took Medicaid, she thought. She dug in her backpack for a stick of gum just as the woman in white got up and went to the water fountain. She looked her over. The dress fit like it was made for her. Classy in an understated way. The Halle Berry haircut was pretty cool, too. *Bet she didn't need Medicaid.*

Nicole popped the gum into her mouth and glanced at the other patient in the room. She reeked of money, and Nicole was pretty sure those sparklers in her ears were the real thing. If she'd had her piece on her she'd definitely wait for Ms. Thing outside.

For an instant, no more than the blink of an eye, the lights seemed to dim and the hum from the air conditioner died down. Nicole figured she'd imagined it.

The nurse stood up from behind the circular desk. "Ladies, I'm terribly sorry, but the doctor has an emergency. She must leave."

"Damn." "What?" "Gimme a break," Tess, Kim, and Nicole chorused.

"I'm really sorry, but babies can't wait." She put on a practiced smile. "I'd be happy to make new appointments for each of you for tomorrow."

Tess jumped up first and marched over to the desk, the spiky heels of her sling-back shoes popping against the polished wood floor. Kim walked up behind her, her pink-tinted lips pinched into a tight thin line. Nicole stood and approached, but kept her distance. The nurse made new appointments, extended more apologies, and they filed out one by one.

"Damn shame," Tess fussed as she stood at the elevator. She finger-fluffed her short bob and moistened her lips with a swipe of her tongue.

Kim didn't respond.

Nicole slung the backpack straps over her shoulders, feeling suddenly shabby and very poor standing next to the two women. "You'd think with all the money we have to pay we'd get better service." She adjusted her halter top over her unbound breasts.

Kim looked at her askance and held her purse a little tighter beneath her arm.

Tess glanced up and watched the lighted dial slowly crawl up the fifteen floors. "If it wasn't so damn hot, I'd walk down. Going down is never the problem, it's getting up." She giggled at her joke, testing the waters.

Nicole snickered.

Kim flushed.

Interesting, Tess observed.

Finally the elevator arrived and the doors silently slid open.

Kim stepped on first and went all the way to the back of the elevator. *The better to watch those two.*

Nicole pressed the button for the lobby. The elevator hesitated a moment, then started down. Tess leaned against the wall and wished she had a cigarette. Ms. Hot Pink would probably have a hissy fit if she lit up. "Nice suit," Tess said to Kim. "Valentino, right?"

Kim's perfectly arched brows rose in surprise. "Yes, it is. Thank you."

Tess smiled. She knew just what she was thinking: What did this heffa know about Valentino? The truth was, she had a suit just like it in fire-engine red. Dorian Eastwood, the actor, bought it for her as a small token of his thanks for "a wonderful evening." She smiled inwardly at the memory.

Nicole adjusted the weight of her backpack. "Elevator is sure taking a long time." She looked up at the dial, which was only on twelve.

Suddenly the elevator dropped, then jerked to a violent halt. They were thrown in opposite directions, and then the metal box went completely black.

CHAPTER TWO

INTRODUCTIONS

"What the . . ." Tess scrambled off her hands and knees and stood on wobbly legs. She rubbed her right hip, the one that had made a major impact on the back wall. She felt around in the dark for the panel and started pressing buttons.

Nothing.

"We're stuck!" Kim said in a cracked voice.

"No shit, Sherlock," Nicole spat. She sat in the corner where she'd been thrown and drew her legs tightly up to her chest. Squinting, she tried to adjust her eyes to the darkness and get a fixed position on the other two women. She didn't want any surprises. Goosebumps rose on her arms.

"Help! Help! Can anyone hear me?" Kim yelled at the top of her voice.

"I can!" Nicole shouted.

"Maybe if we all yelled, someone would get us out of here."

"You watch too much television. You expectin' a white horse to come along with that rescue?" Nicole laughed.

Kim was momentarily stunned into silence, miffed and offended that she should be spoken to that way. "You don't know who you're talking to! Maybe if you'd think about how we can get out of here instead of using what little brain power you have on insults we just might—"

"Say what!" Nicole scrambled to her feet, peering at Kim in the darkness.

Tess felt her way between them. "Just take it easy," she ordered. "Acting like two alley cats in close quarters is totally unproductive."

"My sentiments exactly." Kim gave a haughty lift of her chin.

"I didn't say that to get your approval. What I'm saying is we don't know if this is going to take five minutes or five hours. I'd hate for the lights to come back on and find it's a bloody mess in here." She wished she could see more than the faint whites of their eyes and the pink of Kim's suit. Tess felt a bit of the tension ease in the small space, so she took a cautious step back and listened as the two women moved to their respective corners. *Round one over.*

Tess dug in her purse for her lighter, flicked it on, and held it slightly above her head. She turned slowly in the small space and caught a glimpse of Nicole crouched in the corner and Kim plastered to the wall. She released the lighter and they were all submerged back into darkness.

"Don't they have phones in these things?" Kim asked. "We could call for help."

"Hang on." Tess reached out and felt for the wall panel. She flicked on her lighter again and spotted the phone. She picked it up and listened for a moment. "Dead."

"Great," Nicole muttered. "Now what?" Another series of chills ran up her arms.

"Do you hear anything at all?" Kim stood perfectly still in the hopes of catching some kind of sound of life beyond *those two*. "There's got to be someone out there."

Tess and Nicole listened.

"Nothing," Tess said.

"Not a peep."

"I'll try my cell phone."

"It's not going to work in here," Tess said.

Kim ignored her and fished for her phone in her bag. She flipped it open and started pressing 911, then Stephanie's number and anyone else's she could hit on her speed dial. *Nothing.* At least it was dark, Kim thought, utterly embarrassed when she finally accepted that Tess was right. She shoved the phone back in her purse.

"No luck, huh?" Tess tried to keep the "I told you so," out of her tone.

Kim pursed her lips and didn't respond.

"Well, we'll just have to get comfortable until help comes." Tess took off her sling-back shoes. She slid down onto the floor and thought about her options. There really weren't any. She just had to sit her ass down and wait, try not to suck up too much air, and make sure those two didn't go stir-crazy with her caught in the middle. It was probably some silly technical glitch that would be fixed before they all killed each other anyway.

She'd been dealing with the craziness of women for years: PMS, mood swings, jealousy, ticking biological clocks, self-esteem and self-destructive issues, and everything in between.

And if there was one thing she learned about women, it was that being one didn't mean you really *knew* them. For every woman she met there was something new she learned about womanhood. For the most part, Tess felt she'd learned some pretty good lessons, but there was always room for more. Take these two, for example.

It was apparent, even in the dark, that little Hot Mama was a ride or die chick. She'd caught the look in her eyes when she'd held up the lighter. Hot Mama had some real issues, more than being stuck in the elevator.

As for Ms. High Society, she was simply out of her element, probably never involved in anything more complex or adventurous than getting the wrong dye for her hair.

Tess drew in a breath and tried to get comfortable. She wiggled a bit on the cold, metal floor. Her right cheek was already asleep. She'd give it five more minutes then stand up to get her blood circulating again.

"I can't stay in here!" Kim suddenly said, causing Nicole's head to snap up off her folded arms.

"Doesn't look like you have too much of a choice," Tess replied, "unless you plan on doing some kind of stuntwoman tricks and climbing out. But I don't think it's going to work in that suit."

Nicole snickered to keep from screaming. She was momentarily happy to have some diversion to take her thoughts off the racing of her heart. The small dark box evoked images of her cell when the lights went out. It was the most dangerous time of the day. Then, as now, she kept her back to the wall and her eyes on anything that moved. The only thing close to a weapon she had on her was her house keys. She'd seen how deadly they could be and she'd use them if she had to. Nicole hugged her arms tighter around her body.

The silence was killing her. They'd been stuck for at least two hours, maybe more. She was losing track of time sitting in the dark. The only sounds were those of Kim's sighs and Nicole's muttered curses. She tried to pinpoint the positions of the two women in the darkness. There was no telling how much longer they were going to be stuck, so Tess figured—why not get to know each other? Plus, this would be her opportunity to see if either of them had any potential.

"Since we're here, it would be nice if we knew each other's names, at least. Mine is Tess." She waited a beat.

"Nicole. Everybody calls me Nikki."

Silence.

"Do you have a name you'd like to share, even a nickname?" Tess asked.

Kim hesitated. The last thing she felt like doing was chatting. But sitting in the dark in a box that was getting hotter by the minute was wearing on her, too. Maybe some inane conversation would help.

"Kimberly Sheppard-Benning." Each word was almost spelled out for clarity.

The name immediately registered with Tess. "*The* Kim Sheppard of Sheppard Enterprises?" If there was one thing she prided herself on it was keeping up with the Who's Who. But having clients from Sheppard Enterprises was an added plus in the information column.

"Yes, the same."

"I thought you looked familiar."

"So you're somebody special?" Nicole asked.

Tess bit back a laugh.

Kim couldn't decide if the question was legitimate or another one of Nicole's digs. She chose to ignore it altogether.

"She's the big honcho of the home improvement show, *House Guest*," Tess offered. "And you run a magazine, too."

"Yes, I do."

"Pretty good show, and I actually subscribe to your magazine."

Kim's estimation of Tess rose exponentially. "Thank you."

"What do you do?" Tess asked Nicole.

Nicole wondered what their reaction would be if she told them that her sideline was driving getaway cars and being a lookout for Trust and his boys. If there had been some light in there, she would've loved to have seen the expressions on their faces—especially Ms. Thing; she'd probably faint.

"I'm a receptionist at a dental office." At least she *had been*. Nikki was pretty sure she wouldn't be getting her old job back, but they'd never know that.

Tess gave a little shiver. "Dentists. All I can ever think when I hear that word, is 'ouch.'"

Nicole gave a short laugh. "It's really not that bad. Dentists have been given a bad name."

"With good reason," Tess quipped.

"What's your thing?" Nicole asked.

The corner of Tess's mouth curved into a grin. "I'm a flight attendant." She paused. "And I run a dating service on the side." She waited for their reaction.

"Get out! You mean like an escort thing or a singles thing?"

"More of an *escort* thing." It had been a while since she'd actually told anyone what she really did. For the most part, everyone she met simply thought she was a stewardess who did relatively well for herself. She knew she was taking a chance with these two, but she had her reasons.

"Men actually pay you to go out with them?" Nicole asked, intrigued by the concept.

"Yes, and they pay very well."

Kim was stunned into silence. She was trapped in an elevator with a common hooker! But when she gave herself a moment to think about it, she realized, from the brief time she'd had to look at Tess and hear her speak, she was by no means *common*. She was clearly educated, well-spoken, and she knew the difference between a designer outfit and a knockoff. Her own outfit looked as if it was made for her. She was classy in an "urban" way. She was totally self-assured and confident. No, Tess was no run-of-the-mill hooker.

"I was kidding about the escort thing," Tess said. "Just wanted to lighten things up a little."

"You were joking?" Nicole asked suspiciously.

"Yes, just pulling your leg. But the idea has crossed my mind from time to time. I think it might be kind of interesting."

"Sleeping with all kinds of men? You think that would be interesting?" Kim asked, sounding very offended, her New England accent so sharp that it stung.

"A certain level of man," Tess said in a cool voice. "Class, money, looks." She shrugged. "Just a thought."

Ms. High Society would be a tough one, Tess surmised, as she rubbed the numbness out of her right cheek. But the Latina beauty had possibility.

————

"How long has it been?" Nicole asked into the darkness.

"More than three hours." Kim raked her fingers through her damp hair. "How could anyone not know we're here? This is so unbelievable."

Tess stretched her legs out in front of her on the floor. "Maybe they do and there isn't anything anyone can do about it."

"Whaddya mean?" Nicole asked.

"Maybe it's a major power failure and not just the elevator."

Kim's hand flew to her chest. "You mean a blackout?"

"Exactly."

"A blackout!"

"Yes, a blackout, like the one in 2003. People were trapped all over the city." Many of her clients were forced to spend the night when the mighty city of New York was brought to a grinding halt. A fun time was had by all.

"I do remember the lights dimming and the air conditioning dying down for a second when we were in the doctor's office," Nicole said. "But it happened so fast I thought I'd imagined it."

"That was probably the start of it," Tess said.

"Oh, no." Kim groaned. "That blackout lasted two days in some parts of the city." Her voice rose by two notches. "We can't survive in here for two days."

Nicole squeezed her eyes shut and pressed her forehead against her folded arms. *You can do this*, she silently chanted. *If you can survive solitary, you can do this.* She tossed up a quick prayer to the Holy Mother for added insurance.

"I'm not saying we'll be here for two days, but you have to admit we've been stuck in here for a helluva long time without any sign of help."

"It's so hot." Kim unbuttoned the top two buttons of her suit jacket and wished she hadn't worn stockings.

"We need to stay calm and not move around too much," Tess advised.

"I'm starving," Kim said. "All I had was a yogurt." She laughed nervously.

"I think I got a candy bar in my backpack," Nicole offered. She slipped the straps from around her shoulders and rummaged around inside. "It's a little soft from the heat, but it should be awright." She reached out toward Kim in the darkness. "Here."

Kim swallowed. Her stomach knotted with longing. A half-melted candy bar from that woman? Who knew where it had been? She cleared her throat. "That's okay. No thank you. I'm sure it won't be too much longer."

Nicole emitted a nasty laugh that chilled Kim. "You starvin' but you ain't starvin' enough to take something from me. That right, *puta?*" Nicole stood. "Answer me, bitch!" Long buried, unresolved fury roared through her, beating back her fear of the dark and enclosed places, unspeakable things.

"Get up and say that shit to my face. Tell me you too good to take anything from me!" She shook with rage.

"Hey!" Tess shouted, jumping up. She reached out and grabbed Nicole by the arm. "Relax. She didn't mean anything by it. Did you Kim?" It wasn't a question.

"N–o. I . . . I–I'm allergic to chocolate." She swallowed hard. "Really. That's all. Allergic."

Nicole's chest rose and fell in rapid succession.

"See, it's just an allergy. Nothing personal," Tess said, easing

Nicole back to the other side of the elevator. "Relax," she said in a harsh whisper, feeling Nicole's tremors vibrating through her fingertips.

Nicole snatched her arm away and dropped down to the floor. "Yeah, right," she said through her teeth.

Tess took a breath and retreated to her corner. "Got anything else in that bag?"

"Half bottle of water," she muttered.

"Please, just one swallow," Tess said.

"Sure." Nicole took out the bottle and passed it to Tess.

Tess took a long swallow and sighed as if she were receiving the perfect massage. "I never knew water could taste so good."

Kim licked her lips and nearly choked on the dryness of her throat. But she wouldn't beg.

"You allergic to water?" Nicole asked.

"No."

"Want some?"

"Yes. Thank you."

Tess passed the bottle back to Nicole.

Nicole sat up on her knees and handed the bottle to Kim. "Here. And don't drink it all."

"Thank you." Tentatively Kim brought the bottle to her lips. When was the last time she drank behind someone—a stranger? The thought of it made her stomach rise to her throat. But the overriding need to quench her thirst stamped out any inhibitions and misconceptions she may have had.

"Thank you," she murmured. She took two long swallows and handed the bottle back to Nicole and prayed that she wouldn't catch anything.

———

The trio lapsed into another long silence until Tess's throaty voice slid through the darkness.

"When we were kids my dad used to force my sister and me to go camping in the woods upstate. He insisted it would help our survival skills." She chuckled at the memory. "Anyway, every night, when we sat around in the dark, he would make us tell stories. Sometimes they were funny, or scary, but, no matter what, they always had a way of making us feel better about the trip and each other."

"So you saying we should tell stories, like on a camping trip?" Nicole asked, puzzled.

"Sure. It would certainly kill some time. It might be fun."

Nicole shrugged. "I'm down for just about anything at this point."

"What about you, Kim?" Tess asked.

"I'm sure we'll be out of here soon. I can't imagine that no one knows we're here. They're probably working on getting us out right at this moment." She dabbed at the perspiration dripping from her forehead.

"Is that a yes or a no, Ms. Thing?" Nicole taunted.

"I really don't see the point."

"You wouldn't."

"Look—"

"Hey, I'll go first," Tess interjected, putting a quick halt to the verbal sparring.

Kim huffed.

"It don't have to be a true story, do it?" Nicole asked.

"No. Make it up as you go along. Mix fact with fiction, throw in something spicy, whatever you want."

Nicole nodded. "Cool."

Tess wiggled a bit on the floor. She wasn't sure how much she would reveal and what she would hold back. They probably wouldn't believe her if she told them the truth, anyway.

"Okay." Tess expelled a long breath and plunged in. "My story is about a woman named Tess." She laughed. "One minute she had everything, the next she had nothing, but she was determined to get it all back, one way or another. . . ."

CHAPTER THREE

THE UNUSUAL SUSPECTS

Tess

Tess looked upward. The moon hung over the houses and apartment buildings like a giant orange fireball pressed against a midnight blue sky. A few straggling stars were tossed up against it as if someone had sprinkled a handful of salt for some added flavor. Another scorcher was sure to follow this one, Tess mused. It was the kind of stale, oppressive heat that made the sweat on your arms bubble up over the tiny hairs, making them slick and silky, resembling the kind of "good hair" your grandmother always talked about.

Any other time, Tess would have enjoyed the sight while she sipped on a glass of sparkling Chablis, watching the heavens from the balcony of her midtown Manhattan penthouse with the chill from her air conditioner waiting to wrap her up in cool arms when she stepped back inside. But she wasn't sipping wine, she wasn't on her balcony, and she wasn't in Manhattan on this blistering night. Instead she was sitting on the stoop of a seen-better-days brownstone in the heart of 'do or die Bed-Stuy,' in Brooklyn no less, drinking a lukewarm bottle of Coors.

Music, if you could call it that, blasted from every open window and doorway creating a mind-numbing cacophony of sound on sound. Half-dressed children with kinky hair, braids, afros, and dreads sped up and down the cracked sidewalks and black-tarred streets on rickety bikes hoping to stir up a breeze, if only for a moment. Oversized women inappropriately attired in half-shirts and stretch pants strutted their stuff along the street as if it were the Fashion Avenue runway. Wolf whistles and cat calls from shirtless young men elicited giggles and an extra sway of wide hips.

Tess took a long swallow from the bottle and set it down beside her, then absently wiped the sweat from her forehead with the back of her hand. She was pissed, for lack of a better word. In less than a New York minute her life had taken a three-hundred-and-sixty-degree turn. She'd been on top of the world, and now she was at ground damned zero looking up. A single, angry tear slid down her cheek and hung on the corner of her wide mouth.

This shit wasn't right. It wasn't right at all. She wanted to scream, kick some ass, something. There had to be a way to get it all back. And she would. She didn't spend all that money on her education for nothing. She had friends in high places. Someone would help her. It was simply a matter of calling in a few favors, that's all. Right now she needed to ensure that her ladies were taken care of. A few well-placed calls would cover that. The last thing she needed was one of her ladies turning on her. However, for the time being she needed to lay low. They all understood that.

Tess reached for the damp newspaper that lay on the step beside her and looked at the headline once again.

BIGGEST ESCORT SERVICE ON THE EAST COAST
RAIDED BY VICE SQUAD. MADAM X STILL AT LARGE.

Her eyes narrowed as she studied the face that resembled her own. "Assistant District Attorney Tracy Alexander vows to clean up the city and put all the culprits behind bars," the article stated. "This is just the beginning," said ADA Alexander. "Everyone involved will be apprehended and prosecuted to the fullest extent of the law."

Tess heaved a deep sigh and slowly folded the paper in half and put it back down. "Does that include me, too, sister dear?" Tess murmured.

Not able to take another minute of the scenery or the noise, Tess pulled herself up from her perch and tugged on her shorts before turning to go inside.

"Don't go baby," shouted a male voice from across the street.

Tess took a look over her shoulder, twisted her lips in disgust, and gave him the finger. She wouldn't be caught dead speaking to the likes of him—a sweaty, probably jobless nobody, even if his pecs did look good with no shirt and the bulge in his snug-fitting jeans was a bit more than tempting. She traveled in high circles, filled with wealthy business executives, politicians, actors, movers and shakers. That wannabe didn't have enough money to even get her to say hello. A mere twenty minutes of her time would cost him at least two pairs of his Nike sneakers.

She snorted in dismissal, opened the door and shut it quickly behind her, but not before she caught his parting shout-out.

"You're gonna want me to do that to ya one day!"

His boys roared with laughter.

"You wish," Tess muttered under her breath. She mounted the stairs to her third-floor one-bedroom apartment and pushed away the image of his muscles glistening under the streetlight. The greasy smell of fried everything filled the hallway. "All I want is a way out of this hellhole and I'm going to find it." But when she stepped into the shabby little place that she now called home, all her bravado flew out of the cracked window.

Tess slumped back against the wall. "That's it."

"Say what?" Nicole squawked. "That's it? What happened?"

"Not sure yet. I'm still working the rest of it out in my head."

"How much truth was in that story?" Kim asked.

"Depends on what you're willing to believe."

"I feel cheated," Nicole said, sucking her teeth in mild annoyance.

"Can you do better?" Kim challenged.

Nicole cut her a look in the dark. "You're damned right. I got plenty of stories."

"I'm sure you do. Why don't you try to entertain us with one of them?"

"You know if you ever come through my neighborhood—"

"Highly unlikely."

"Ladies, ladies, and I'm starting to use the term loosely, we're all hot, hungry, tired, and maybe a little scared. And I don't know about everyone else, but I have to pee. For the time being we're stuck with each other. Relax." Tess waited a beat. "Okay, Ms. Nikki, you think you can top my story?"

"I know I can."

"Let's hear it then."

Nicole cleared her throat. "Well, see, there was this chick

and she was just getting released from jail. But she didn't do nothin'. It was all a big mistake. Anyway . . ."

Nikki

The chilling clang of metal against metal vibrated through Nicole Perez's teeth, settling in her head with the force of an anvil dropped from a third-floor tenement window. For eighteen months that sound filled every fiber of her being, and if she lived to be one hundred she would never stop hearing it in her dreams.

Nicole held her meager belongings tightly against her chest—nothing much, but it was hers. Her waist-length ponytail swung behind her as she followed the armed guard down the dull gray corridor, keeping her eyes lowered so as not to make contact with the poor souls trapped in their steel cages.

"Sign here," the guard ordered when they finally reached the front desk.

She did as she was told and signed her name on the blank line.

"I'm sure we'll see you again," the guard said, giving her a smile that turned her stomach. "We always do."

Nicole clenched her jaws to keep from spitting out something that would give him an excuse to send her back. She slid the clipboard across the table.

The guard led the way to the exit and suddenly Nicole was terrified. True, it had been horrific inside. She'd seen things and had things done to her that nightmares are made of, but the outside was now the enemy. Any misstep and she would be right back here doing the max. She'd rather die.

"Be seeing ya," the guard chuckled as the final gate swung open.

Nicole stepped out into the world, sucked in a lungful of free air, and wept. For several moments she stood in place as if her sneakered feet had been magically cast in cement while the tears flowed down her cheeks.

A gentle hand cupped her shoulder.

She looked up at her older brother through the film of her tears and quickly wiped her face with a balled fist. "Thanks for coming, *hijo*."

Ricky nodded, put his arm around her waist, and drew her close. "Come on, sis, let's go home," he said gently.

Nicole hesitantly allowed herself to find comfort in her brother's embrace without trembling with dread. For months the thought of anyone touching her, coming near her, in her space, put her on alert. Every waking minute she had to be on point. If she let her guard down for an instant . . . She didn't want to think about it. Once was enough to last her into the next eternity.

She'd learned quickly that in there she wasn't a person with a soul or emotions. She was number 8687988 to the guards and a too-pretty face for her own damned good to the other women who wanted to scar her inside and out. She'd learned to hold her own, to not take any crap from anyone. In time, she gained the respect due her. She owed her resilience to the lessons she'd learned on the street—back in Brooklyn—riding fast cars with even faster guys who didn't have time for excuses or female whining.

Nicole stared out the passenger-side window. The car picked up speed and the prison slowly receded into the background. She leaned her head back against the seat and closed her eyes.

"Everybody's looking forward to having you back home," Ricky said.

"Everybody?" She thought about Trust—the reason why she

had done the time. Not once since she was locked up had he come to see her. How would he react now that she was home?

"Yes, your sister. I know you ain't thinking about that bastard Trust," he snapped, as a frown creased his caramel-colored brow. "He's nothing but trouble, and if you want to stay out of it, stay away from him. I'm warning you, Nikki."

Nicole folded her arms and stared out the window. She knew her brother was right. Her on-again, off-again relationship with Trust had been a constant roller coaster ride—from the fights, to the women that clung to him like he was flypaper, to the things he asked her to do. She knew they were wrong, dangerous, but she wanted to please him, prove to him and to herself that she was better, tougher than those other *putas* that vied for his time. She lived for the excitement, the thrill, even though much of it was illegal. The more dangerous the job, the more she tingled inside. It was like a high and just as addictive. What was she going to do to kick the habit?

Nicole swallowed hard and waited for the verdict.

"So . . . what happened? Did she go back to that guy?" Kim asked, surprising both Nicole and Tess with her sudden interest.

Nicole's tone was quiet and thoughtful. "She's still trying to figure that part out."

"What did she go to jail for?" Tess asked gently.

Nicole sniffed and wiped away the tears from her eyes, for once thankful for the dark.

"Accessory to a robbery. I . . . she drove the getaway car." A nervous chuckle slipped across her lips. "Good story, huh?"

"Pretty good," Tess said, "had me hooked. But I'm like Kim, I want to know what she does about that guy Trust. Sounds to me like he needs to be taught a lesson—the hard way. Maybe if we sit here long enough we'll figure something out."

"Let's hope not. I mean not about the story . . . sitting here," Kim said.

"So what about you Ms. TV Star? I know you have tons of stories." Tess squirmed a bit on the hard floor, in desperate need of a cigarette.

"Not really."

"Come on. We did it," Nicole challenged.

"I . . . what would I talk about?"

"Whatever you want. Your fantasy, whatever. Fact or fiction, or a healthy combination of both," Tess said.

Kim ran her tongue across her dry lips and took a short breath. "Okay . . . but my story will be *all* fiction."

"Fine," Tess and Nicole chorused.

"And since you're last, it should be the best of the bunch," Tess added.

For the first time Kim had a hint of laughter in her voice. "Great, no pressure."

"Nope, not at all."

Kim suddenly felt a giddy excitement that she couldn't explain. "Okay. My story starts off in a law office . . ."

Kimberly

Kimberly Sheppard-Benning clasped her hands tightly in her lap as she listened to her attorney, John Weinstein, explain the tragedy that was rapidly becoming her life. She gave a stoic lift of her chin. How could she have let this happen? She wasn't a stupid woman and she should have known that if her greedy, insecure husband, Troy, were to ever discover her infidelity he would leap on it like a hungry man gobbling his last meal.

"Troy wants you to step down as CEO of Sheppard Enterprises and turn it over to him," John said. He glanced up at his client over his half-framed glasses. "What in the hell happened, Kim? This seems to have come out of nowhere and Troy is not budging." He snatched off his glasses and placed them on the desk next to the opened file.

"What can I do to stop him?" She tapped her nails against her purse.

"You can fight this, of course. The company is yours. There's no question about that. You started that company before your marriage to Troy. I really don't understand how he thinks he can get away with this. This is New York, not California."

Kimberly swallowed. She knew exactly how he could get away with it. She looked John directly in the eye. "I need to explain some things to you, John, in the strictest confidence," she said in her clipped, New England accent.

"Of course."

By rote, she raked her fingers through her shoulder-length blond hair, showcasing the sparkling diamond studs that were her signature piece of jewelry.

"About four years ago . . . I became involved with someone."

John's brows rose but he remained silent.

Kimberly cleared her throat. "Someone who is married to a very important person . . . in government. Troy found out about the affair."

"And he threatened to tell all?"

Her ocean blue eyes did not waver. "Yes."

John rubbed his hand across the five o'clock shadow on his chin. "He has you over a barrel, Kim, if you're unwilling to let go of everything. That's pretty clear." He paused. "What do you want to do?"

"Have him killed," she said, as calmly as if she were noting an item on the grocery list.

John chuckled. "Right."

"Well, I won't have him take everything that I've worked for, everything that I've built, ruin me, and the person I love, because he is too lazy and greedy to do anything on his own." She sat taller in the expensive leather chair. "I made him. I can break him and I need you to help me do that."

"Kim . . . I . . . ."

She stood and picked up her purse. "I pay you to handle my affairs, John. So please do what I pay you for." She turned to leave.

John jumped up from his seat, his face beet red. "Kim, you're being unreasonable. Getting . . . rid of—ruining people is not what you pay me to do."

She glanced at him over her right shoulder. "It is now."

Kimberly got behind the wheel of her onyx Jaguar and slid on her sunglasses against the glare of the setting sun. John would do as instructed or she would find a way to do it herself. There was no way that she was going to allow Troy to reveal her relationship with Stephanie. It would not only ruin her lover, but any chances of Stephanie's husband, Malcolm's, re-election bid for congress.

She pressed the speed dial on her cell. Moments later, Stephanie Abrams's voice came through the car's speakers.

"It's me. We need to talk," Kim said. "Can you meet me tomorrow evening about six at our usual place?"

Kim was trembling with an odd exhilaration, having spoken the words out loud. But what if they heard the truth in her little tale of retribution? She smiled to herself. She didn't care if they did.

For several moments, the odd trio sat perfectly still. In the silence they could still hear the echo of their own stories as well as each other's. How much was true only the teller knew for certain. But one thing was clear, even in the dark, they'd crossed an invisible line and there was no turning back.

Perhaps it was the darkness that acted as some kind of shield, a protective cloak that wrapped around them and gave them the courage to say the words they'd never share in the light of day. The darkness made them bold and fearless. Besides, they were three strangers and probably would never see each other again.

"Helluva story," Tess finally said, breaking the silence.

"Yeah." Nicole hugged her knees a bit tighter. She peered into the darkness, wondering if Kim really did have a thing for women, or was it all a lie? And was she really planning on bumping off her husband?

Tess swallowed over the dry knot in her throat. She knew that every word she'd uttered had been true, and all her instincts told her that the other stories were based in fact, as well. She'd opened a Pandora's box. There were things brewing deep inside these women that needed to get out and leaped at the chance she'd offered. And as different as they were, they were all in the same boat—their lives in upheaval and each looking for a way to repair the damage and regain what was rightfully theirs.

"What if there was a way to get it all back?" Tess asked. "I'm not saying that the things that were said are true—but what if they were?" She let the question hang in the heaviness of the air.

Kim laughed. "Don't you think you're taking this story-telling thing too far?"

"Yeah, it was all made up," Nicole asked more than stated.

"I know if I had the chance to get back what I'd lost I'd take it," Tess said without hesitation.

"Easier said than done," Kim murmured as she pondered an untimely demise of her husband.

Trust needed to pay for what happened to her, Nicole thought. He had no idea how she'd suffered, what she'd lost, and never once did he come and see about her. She wanted him to hurt as badly as she did—after she slept with him once more for old time's sake.

"No one has the right to take away what someone else has worked for, sacrificed to attain," Tess said, with the assurance of one who knows answers that others can only guess. "Whether it's a business, a relationship, your freedom, or your pursuit of happiness—whatever it may be, and then use what they've taken for their own personal gain." She waited a beat to let her words sink in. "True, we've only known each other for a few hours—although at times it felt like an eternity," she quipped. "But all that aside, our similarities outweigh our differences."

"What are you suggesting?" Kim asked. "If, of course, our little stories were true."

Tess smiled in the dark. "I'm suggesting that the strength of who we are individually can be multiplied by banding together. Going it alone is never easy. But knowing that someone you can trust has your back makes the battle easier to fight."

"You mean like a support system," Nicole said.

"Exactly. Someone to bounce your plans off of, share information with, use their connections to help all of us."

"Why would we want to do that, especially with perfect strangers?" Kim asked.

"Because someone who has nothing else to lose can be your best ally. Each of us has skills and resources that the others don't."

"Like what?" Kim asked, sounding insulted by the implication, unable to fathom what either of those two women could have that she would want.

"Think about it, Kim, you hire perfect strangers every day based on what they tell you they have accomplished and what they can bring to the table to help you achieve your goals. You take a chance. What do they have to gain? More than they have to lose if they do a good job. Take you, for example. You have media and money contacts—corporate power and legitimacy. Nicole has street savvy and connections with a side of life that would be totally out of our grasp to obtain. Information and resources on the street are often more reliable than an FBI team of experts."

Nicole chuckled. "Seems like you left someone out of the playbook."

"Me . . . I have the power of charm and persuasion, the ability to zero in on what people need. I know how to use what I have to get what I want and convince you that you want it, too. It's what I do. Just like Nicole can move with ease outside of our circle and you, Kim, operate within a system that would never accept me or Nikki."

Nicole and Kim were quiet as they contemplated the veracity of Tess's analysis. Everything she said was true, right on target, if they accepted the notion that even half of what they confessed was reality.

Tess made one final pitch. "We have plenty to lose if we sit back and let it happen, but we have much more to gain if we all work together. I don't believe that any of us are the kind of women who allow life to beat us down. If we were, we wouldn't have gotten this far."

Suddenly the elevator jerked, rumbled, and came to life. The lights flickered, died, then dimly came on.

The three women pulled themselves up off the floor, each looking the worse for wear. They glanced at each other, then quickly looked away, suddenly uncomfortable in each other's presence.

"Anybody in there?" a male voice shouted.

"Yes. Yes," the women yelled in unison.

"Just hang on a bit longer. You're stuck in between floors. We're going to have to hoist you out from the hatch."

"Oh, God," Kim moaned.

"Looks like we'll get out of here, after all," Tess said, wishing she'd had a few more minutes to work her magic.

Moments later, there were sounds of heavy footsteps above and the hatch was pried open. The beam of a flashlight illuminated the semi-darkness and a fireman stuck his head down.

"Everybody okay?"

"As well as can be expected," Kim said.

"How many of you are stuck in there?"

"Three of us," Nicole answered.

"I'm going to lower a rope. You're going to have to climb up to me."

The elevator suddenly shook and the trio screamed.

"Relax. But I want you to get out of there as quickly as possible. Okay."

A thick knotted rope was dropped down into the elevator. "One at a time. Grab on tight and I'll pull you up."

"You go first," Nicole said to Kim.

"I—I can't."

"Yes, you can," Tess said, pushing her toward the rope. "We'll help you."

After several attempts, Kim finally held on to the rope and was pulled up into the shaft. Nicole was next, followed by Tess.

They emerged into more darkness.

"Okay, listen, the door above us has been pulled open. There are a set of metal stairs against that wall." He shined the flashlight on the steps.

"Those aren't stairs," Kim wailed, looking at the threatening pieces of metal.

"Well, they're as close to stairs as we're going to get. You need to climb up to the floor above."

The elevator shook and vibrated. The women grabbed each other to keep from getting thrown to the floor, or worse, down the shaft.

"Listen to me, ladies. The power could come on at any minute. If it does, there's no telling what this elevator will do— go up, or down." He looked from one to the other. "Let's not be here to find out. Come on." He inched over to the wall and helped them up the metal rungs.

"We used to do this all the time in the projects," Nicole said, trying to sound brave as she inched her way up. Sometimes they did it for fun, sometimes out of necessity. She knew exactly what he meant about not wanting to be in the shaft if the elevator started up. Some nights, she could still hear her neighbor Felix's scream as he fell down fourteen floors. "Just don't look down."

That is exactly what Kim did and the world suddenly swayed beneath her.

Tess grabbed the back of Kim's suit jacket. Kim scraped and flailed to get a grip back on the railing. The fireman latched onto Tess to keep them both from following Kim's purse, sailing down into the darkness.

Kim held onto Tess like a wounded child to its mother. Her body shook uncontrollably as she whimpered that she couldn't do it.

"It's okay," Tess soothed. "You're okay."

"What happened?" Nicole yelled, imagining the worst.

"We're okay," the fireman shouted back. "Keep going." He turned to Tess and Kim. "I'm going to go up with you," he said to Kim, speaking to her as you would to a child. "One step at a time."

Kim violently shook her head against Tess's shoulder until the fireman had to pry her away.

"You can do it, Kim," Nicole shouted. "You have to. We have business to take care of. Can't do it without you."

Kim sniffed hard then slowly nodded her head. The fireman put his arm around Kim's waist as he eased her up.

Tess was left alone in the darkness. "Damn," she murmured, as she felt her way up the rail by the sliver of light from the flashlight. "Double damn."

They were greeted in the lobby by several firemen who

quickly ushered them outside after checking to make sure they were all right.

"What's happened?" Tess asked. "We've been stuck in there for hours."

"Blackout," one fireman said. "The whole city, all the way upstate. I hope you ladies have on your walking shoes. There're no trains or buses." He extended his arm toward the front door. "As you can see, traffic is a mess."

When they stepped outside it was pure bedlam. Car horns were furiously honking as the signal lights were still inoperable. Office buildings were wrapped in darkness.

"Wow, you were right," Nicole said as she walked to the street on shaky legs.

"I wish I wasn't." Tess looked around at the mayhem of stranded citizens heading for bridges leading home or just a place to lay their heads. "How are we going to get out of here?"

"My car is parked in the lot about a block away," Kim said in a voice that still shook.

"You'll never make it home in this traffic."

"I'm certainly not going to spend the night here." She wrapped her arms around her body.

"You might not have a choice."

"We could walk," Nicole offered.

"Maybe *you* could," Tess said, noting Nicole's low-heeled sandals, "but not in our shoes."

Kim heaved a sigh. "What do you suggest?" she asked, then realized that she was actually asking Tess for advice.

"Maybe we can find a hotel room or something, at least un-til morning."

Kim brightened, shoving aside her embarrassment for her earlier behavior and stepping into a realm that she could control. "I have a standing room at the Sheraton on Seventh Avenue. There's only one bed but it does have a pull-out couch."

"Sounds like a plan to me. There's no way I'm walking to Brooklyn and it would take me the rest of the night to drive home in this mess. Are you okay with that Nikki?"

Nicole glanced at Kim. "If it's all right with you."

"We've already spent more than six hours together. A few more won't kill us." She swallowed what was left of her pride. "I–I'm really sorry for losing it like that. It's just—"

"Hey, forget it," Nicole said. "Everybody got something that freaks them out." She gave her a crooked smile.

Kim looked at Nicole for a moment and nodded her head, understanding exactly what she meant.

"Let's start walking," Tess said.

Almost an hour later they arrived at the Sheraton. The lobby was packed with bodies. The hotel staff was scurrying around frantically trying to appease everyone who came through the door. The line to the registration desk wrapped around the dimly lit interior. Full power had obviously not been restored. The place felt like a sauna.

Kim straightened her shoulders and tried to brush out the wrinkles in her suit. She ran her fingers through her hair. "Follow me." She pushed past the swelling crowd and made her way to the front desk, ignoring the man in front of her.

"Kimberly Sheppard," she said to the flustered desk clerk. "I want my regular room and a cot brought upstairs as well."

The desk clerk looked up at Kim without an iota of recognition. "Ms.—as you can see we are quite overwhelmed tonight. You'll have to wait on line like everyone else. I—"

Kim's cheeks flamed red and it wasn't from the heat. "It's apparent that you don't know who I am." Her New England accent was in full force. "I pay an incredible amount of money to this hotel to have a room ready at my disposal. I'm sure you can make whatever concessions are necessary to see that my room is made available." She glared at his name tag. "Mr. Reynolds."

"Ms. Sheppard—"

Tess stepped up next to Kim. "Sir," she put on her winning smile and reached across the desk to cover his hand with hers, making tiny circles with her finger in the center of his palm. His nostrils flared. "Mrs. Sheppard-Benning is very tired. We all are. I'm sure you want to keep one of your best customers happy," she said in a throaty whisper. "It wouldn't do the hotel any good if word got out that you turned one of the hotel's major benefactors away or somehow your misstep wound up in her magazine." She paused and turned to Kim with a questioning expression on her face. "Don't you do a regular piece on places to stay in New York?" She smiled benignly then turned to the clerk. "Whatever you can do would be greatly appreciated."

He cleared his throat. "Do you have any identification?" he asked, a bit absently, growing aroused by what Tess was doing to him.

Kim glared at him. "Mr. Reynolds, my identification, along with my credit cards and drivers license, is at the bottom of an elevator shaft, which is where I would be if it weren't for these two women! Get me my room."

His Adam's apple bobbed up and down as recognition finally set in. Tess released his hand. He turned to the computer, realized it was useless without power, and pulled out a guest register. "You have no idea how many people we've had to turn away tonight," he murmured, flipping open the book. After several minutes he looked up. He lowered his voice. "Someone will take you upstairs and get the door open. Suite 1509, your usual room. The elevators are still out," he apologized. "You'll have to walk. He went beneath the desk, opened a metal box and removed a master key. He signaled for a bellhop and handed him the key. "Please escort Mrs. Benning and her guests to the suite on fifteen." He slid the key across the desk and turned weary, red-rimmed eyes on Kimberly. "I'm terribly sorry. But I'm sure you understand how—"

Tess patted his hand. "No apology is necessary. Thank you." She winked. He swallowed hard.

The trio, led by the bellhop, wound their way around the throng and finally made it to the stairwell and began the long walk up fifteen floors.

"Nice work," Nicole said. "The look on his face was priceless."

Kim huffed.

"Sometimes the way to calm the savage beast is with a little honey," Tess said.

By the time they reached the fifteenth floor they had moved beyond exhaustion.

The bellhop stuck the key into the lock and pushed the door open. He stood aside as the women filed in. "Will there be anything else?" he asked.

"No. Thank you," Kim said. She lowered her voice. "Anyone have money for a tip? My purse . . ."

"Two bucks cool?" Nicole asked.

Kim started to make a comment, but Tess saw it coming.

"Two dollars is fine, Nikki," Tess said.

Nicole handed the bellhop two damp, crumpled dollar bills and shut the door behind him.

Kim grimaced. "I'll get some candles. Make yourselves comfortable." She went into the kitchen and took out a box of candles. "You still have that lighter?" she called out.

Tess took the lighter out of her purse, flicked it on, and found Kim. She began lighting the candles.

"There are candleholders in the living room."

"Okay."

"Where's the bathroom?" Nicole asked, her bladder ready to burst.

"Down the hall on your left."

"Here, take this." Tess handed her a candle.

"Thanks."

Kim left them both and walked into her bedroom. Tess followed.

Even in the semi-darkness she could tell the place had style. This was the atmosphere she was accustomed to, lush and expensive. She had no doubt that Kim Sheppard had good taste, this suite only verified what she already knew.

"You live well," Tess said, standing in the doorway.

Kim turned toward her. "Thank you."

"I did, too, once upon a time." She stepped into the room and ran her hand along the smooth surface of the winter white armoire.

"Once upon a time?"

"Long story." She smiled. "Maybe if we get stuck in an elevator again, I'll tell you all about it."

Kim looked at her for a long moment. "It is true, isn't it?"

The corner of Tess's mouth lifted halfway. "Is what true?"

"The story you told us in the elevator."

Tess's right brow arched in question. "Is yours?"

Kim turned away. "What if it is?"

"If it is, then maybe we can find a way to help each other." She stepped closer.

"Help each other? How could you possibly help me and what in the world can I do for you?"

Nicole walked into the room. "Help each other do what?"

Kimberly lifted her chin. "Anyone want a drink? I know I could use one." She left the bedroom, breezing by Tess and Nicole, and went to the wet bar in the living room. From behind the counter she took out three oversized goblets. She glanced up and smiled at their wide-eyed expressions. "After the day we've had, we deserve it." She took out a bottle of brandy.

"Is anybody gonna answer my fuckin' question?" Nicole glared from one woman to the next.

"Must you always be so vulgar? You're much too beautiful to have such a filthy mouth," Kim replied, matter of fact. She

shoved a glass in Nicole's direction. "You could go so much further with just a little bit of class."

Something ugly was on the tip of her tongue but Nicole
washed it down with the amber liquid instead, letting the burn
consume the constant rage boiling inside her. It wouldn't take
away a night's sleep to blow her away, she thought. She plopped
down in an available chair.

Tess crossed the room and took her drink from Kim.
"Thanks." She took a sip. "Hmmm, good stuff."

A look of admiration filled Kim's eyes. She could always appreciate someone who had taste.

Tess sat on the love seat and stretched her legs out in front
of her. She took a swallow of her drink. "What happened today
happened for a reason," she said slowly.

"What do you mean?" Kim asked from behind the bar.

"We got stuck together because we were supposed to. Let's
be real. What are the chances of the three of us ever crossing
each other's paths? None."

"So what?" Nicole muttered. "Three strangers meet up and
talk shit in an elevator." She finished off her drink, went to the
bar and refilled her glass. She stared at Kim. "Good stuff."

Kim ignored her.

The light from the candles danced in the darkness, casting
long shadows against the white walls, giving the room a surreal
feel.

"Once we admit that the things we said back there are true,
then we can help each other get what's ours," Tess continued.
"If either of you are willing to take the risk, we can make it
happen."

"Make what happen?" Nicole asked.

"Make our problems go away for good, dole out the retribution that's deserved, and get back what is rightfully ours."

Kim shook her head in dismissal. "Don't be ridiculous."

"Why ridiculous? Be honest. Haven't you thought how much easier your life would be if your husband was out of the way? And haven't you spent sleepless nights praying for that man of yours to pay for what he's done, but didn't know how to get away with it? Hasn't everyone in some dark corner of their mind wondered what it would be like to pull off the perfect crime?"

She waited for dissenting voices and got none. She smiled to herself. "I could use another drink." She got up and went to the bar. Kim refilled her glass.

"I'll be the first to admit it," Tess said, taking a long swallow. "Everything I told you in that elevator is true. There, I've confessed. Less than a month ago, I was relaxing in my penthouse. I had clothes, cars, more money than I could ever spend, a thriving enterprise. I entertained, traveled. Now I'm stuck in a four-story walk-up in the middle of Brooklyn, with the scent of garbage floating up to my window. Everything is gone and if my sister has her way, she'll see me spend the next few years in jail. I can't let that happen."

Kim finished her drink and refilled her glass. She walked around the bar with the bottle and refilled Tess's and Nicole's glasses, then sat down on the carpeted floor.

"If my husband has his way, I'll lose everything," Kim said, finding confidence in the glass and the dark. "I can't let *that* happen and I can't let him hurt Stephanie."

"So you really do have a thing with a woman," Nicole said, more curiosity than rancor in her voice.

"Yes."

They were quiet for a moment.

The pain in Nicole's voice pierced the silence. "They raped me in there. They hurt me . . . bad." Her voice hitched. "And he never came, never called. He could have stopped it all from happening if he would have told the truth, but he didn't and I couldn't." She finished off her drink and stuck her glass out for a refill.

"Do you always have to look like you have a stick up your ass every time I open my mouth?" Nicole asked, seeing the pinched expression on Kim's face.

Tess nearly spit out a mouthful of her drink.

Shock blazed in Kim's blue eyes. "Perhaps if I was more accustomed to the vulgarity that is apparently you, it wouldn't bother me," Kim snapped, attempting to hide her horror at Nicole's confession behind a veneer of chilling indifference. Kim tossed down her napkin. "This was not a good idea." She got up and refilled her glass.

Kim was so disturbed her hands shook. Ugly images and memories that wouldn't die danced in her head. Violation of women in any form appalled her, with violation by men heading the list. But any words of sympathy she may have offered were obliterated by Nicole's attack on her.

Never had she been spoken to in such a manner. She didn't tolerate it from her employees and she certainly wouldn't tolerate it from this . . . this . . . she couldn't find the words. This was not her life, not the people she was accustomed to being with. If there was even a modicum of truth to their stories, then she was in the company of a prostitute and a felon. Nothing in her sterile, white-collar life prepared her for this. What had she gotten herself into? She should toss them both out, now.

"You feel like you're out of your element, don't you?" Tess asked.

Kim cut her gaze in Tess's direction.

Tess took a long breath. "You're accustomed to running things, to saying the word and it's done, being in charge. So am I and in Nicole's world so is she. What we have are three chiefs and no Indians."

The tight lines around Kim's mouth and eyes gradually eased.

"We're intelligent women. We wouldn't have gotten to where we are otherwise. So there has to be a way for the three of us to put our differences aside and concentrate on the common denominator." She looked from one to the other. "Retribution. We all want the same thing."

Kim took a quick sip of her drink. She wanted to guzzle it down and take another. That's the kind of mood she was in.

"Can we at least agree that our objectives are the same?" By degrees, Kim and Nicole nodded in turn.

"Good. Maybe I should go first and break the ice." She took two long sips of her drink, then set it down. "Just so that we're clear, everything I said on the elevator is true. I'm Madam X and have been for the past eighteen years." She paused. "Someone has decided to put an end to my business. It started with a phone call that my assistant took about three weeks ago telling me I might have about forty-eight hours at best to get out before we were raided. The warrants had already been issued."

"Whoa," Nikki murmured.

"I had to dismantle my entire business in a matter of hours, contact all the women, close up the houses in Harlem and in Cape May and destroy any incriminating documents."

"I'm sure you had your contingency plan in place long ago, in the event that something like this ever happened." Kim stated, more than asked.

"Doesn't every good businesswoman?" She gave Kim a wink.

Suddenly, Nicole jumped up, knocking over her drink. "You two think you're such hot shit with your fancy talk, your fancy clothes, and your business plans!" She glared at Tess and Kim with contempt twisting her features. "You wouldn't last ten minutes in my world. You think you better than me, but you ain't. You ain't nothin'" she cried. Tears spilled from her eyes in concert with the amber liquid that seeped into the white carpet. "I'm somebody, too." She pounded on her chest before turning away and stumbling down the semi-darkened hallway.

Moments later the bathroom door slammed shut.

Nicole stared at her reflection in the flickering candlelight. She hated them. Hated women like them who thought they were better because of the clothes they wore and their zip codes. They reminded her of what she could never be but desperately wanted to claim.

Kim and Tess exchanged bleary-eyed looks.

"If it wasn't for chance and opportunity, how much different would we be from Nicole?" Tess stated more than asked. She drained her glass.

The hard knock of conscience nudged Kim in the ribs. Finally she got up and went to tap on the bathroom door.

"Nicole." She pounded on the door. "It's me. Kim. The white woman you hate and whose alcohol you are consuming," she managed to say in slurred suburban.

"Leave me alone."

Kim heard the toilet flush.

"Listen," she paused to brace herself against the door. "Do you really think we're better than you?"

"Hell no!" she shouted through the door.

"Exactly. Look, I know I can be a little condescending sometimes. It's just who I am. Nothing personal, I can assure you. I'm like that with everyone," she admitted, and was momentarily taken aback realizing that what she said was actually true. She lowered her voice. "I won't even mention what I thought about Tess." She snickered and heard Nicole chuckle.

The bathroom door opened and Nicole stood in the threshold. She wiped her face with the back of her hand.

"There's a box of Kleenex on the sink," Kim said, hiding the displeasure she felt at watching such an uncouth act. "You really don't have to use your hands."

Nicole planted her hand on her hip, almost tipped over, but quickly regained her balance. "Do you practice being a bitch or does it come natural?"

Kim didn't flinch. "It's hard work, but someone has to do it."

Nicole looked at Kim for a moment, shook her head, and followed Kim back into the living room.

"So where were we before I flipped?" Nicole asked, plopping down on the floor.

"I was talking about my narrow escape," Tess replied. "I came to the doctor's office to . . . assess some new possibilities."

Kim's blue eyes widened. "You came to the doctor's office to recruit more women?" Kim didn't know if she was flattered or insulted.

The corner of Tess's mouth flickered into a grin. "That was

the original idea. But I thought better of it. My first instinct was to kick the past to the curb and start new—all over again. Then it hit me; why should I?" She glanced from one to the other. I spent a good part of my womanhood on my back. I want to go out on my feet. And in order to do that I need to meet my challenges face to face. Think what you want of me, but I never hurt anyone. Which is more than can be said of the people who did this, not only to me, but to both of you. And we can either sit back and take it, or get what is due to us, what we've earned.

"I have a Masters Degree in Economics and a B.A. in Business. I figure all that scholing combined with life lessons should be worth something," Tess added, and finished off her drink.

Kim frowned. "Then why—"

Tess's cool brown eyes slid in Kim's drection. "A first, it was a means to pay for the education everyone and their mama said I needed to have to survive in this world—*and* to keep up with my sister. But as time passed, I realized that I was putting book knowledge to work. I was a businesswoman and what I do is a business—with perks. Simple as that." She shrugged. "The only reason there are laws against what I do is because the government is pissed that it misses out on taxes. No more, no less. But the funny thing is, it's the politicians, businessmen, and decision makers who are our regular guests. It was a judge who tipped me off about the raid."

Tess's gaze drifted off.

Nicole thought about her own twisted life, orchestrated at the hands of someone else. "What are you going to do when you find them?"

Tess grinned.

"I know what *I* want to do," Nicole said, the bitterness evident in the bite of her words. "I want them to go through exactly what I did, only worse. I want them to live in fear every time they close their eyes, never knowing if they're going to see the next damned day."

"You never did say how you wound up in jail," Kim said in that condescending tone of hers.

Nicole cut her eyes in Kim's direction, fixed her mouth to say something smart, but realized that Kim just didn't know any better. "I was stupid . . . in love with a man who would turn on his own mother for the right price. And when it all went down, he left me out there to take the weight."

Kim frowned and shook her head in confusion. "What does that mean?"

Tess bit back a smirk and translated. "She took the responsibility for something someone else did and the man who should have been there for her turned his back on her." She looked at Nicole. "Is that about right?"

Nicole nodded.

"Oh," Kim murmured, feeling as if she'd just listened to a conversation in another language.

Nicole turned to Tess. "How can you help me?" she demanded, more than asked. "You seem to have all the big ideas. If it was left up to me, I'd just go in there and blow them all away." Her perfect face twisted into a grimace of anger.

"That's not the way."

Nicole slammed her hand down on the table, thinking of what happened to her one night too many. "Then, what is?"

Tess turned to Kim. "Are you in or are you out?"

Kim knew without a doubt that she could never allow her other life to become public. She had no idea short of disposing of her husband how to keep that from happening. Humph, maybe Nicole really was the answer. She had enough money to pay Nicole whatever she wanted to do the job, and she didn't seem to have any qualms about getting her hands dirty. After all, she was a convicted felon.

Kim gave a short nod of her head in agreement.

"Good," Tess said. She leaned forward and lowered her voice. "This won't work if anyone slips up. One action is intricately tied to the next. And always remember, the mark rarely suspects the ones who are a part of their agenda . . ."

By the time the second bottle of brandy was finished, the three women shared stories of their early beginnings, their struggles and triumphs. Most importantly, they shared the minute details of the objects of their hatred, their habits, hangout spots, associates. They laughed, they cried, they drank some more, wallowing in their anger and misery, that dark, untapped place in their souls buoyed by the power of one common objective—retribution.

"I have an idea," Tess slurred.

"No more ideas from you," Nicole said, her accent thick and stilted. She giggled.

"Gimme a piece of paper, Kim."

Kim looked at Tess through bleary eyes. "Not . . . getting up . . . get it yourself. Next to the bed." She leaned her head back against the seat of the couch and closed her eyes.

Tess pushed herself up off the floor with the help of a good shove from Nicole and stumbled into the bedroom. She sat down on the bed and opened the nightstand drawer.

On each of three slips of paper she wrote a single name,

stuck them in separate envelopes, then sealed the envelopes.

"Tell you what," she said, reentering the living room, her words trailing behind her in slow motion. "I'm going to put these envelopes on the bar. Everybody gets one."

"What's in 'em?" Nicole asked. "Money?" She snickered.

"The name of the person you have to kill, silly."

Kim burst out laughing and slapped her thigh. "Like a Secret Santa!" She cracked up laughing again.

"I know my vision is kinda cloudy, but I can count. That's four envelopes." Nicole frowned. "Who else is playing?"

"The fourth one is blank." She looked at them. "One of us may be lucky enough to get it." Tess waited a beat. "It's like a game of Russian Roulette. Who wants to play? Who's woman enough? Who wants to make them pay for screwing up our lives?"

"I do!" Nicole managed to get up off the floor and staggered over to the counter. She stared at the envelopes. After several moments of indecision she picked one and returned to her space on the couch. She stared at Kim. "Well, whatchu waiting for, Christmas?" She jerked her chin toward the counter. "Maybe you'll get lucky and get the blank one. You don't have the heart to do anything bigger than signing checks for the leech husband of yours anyway." She started to laugh and could not stop.

"Fuck you!" Kim said, with such regal elocution it shut Nicole up in midchuckle.

Tess covered her mouth but it didn't stop the burst of laughter. "Didn't think you had it in you."

Kim walked to the counter with as much dignity as she could summon and snatched up an envelope without a second thought. She tossed Nicole a look of triumph with a haughty lift of her chin.

"Guess that leaves me." The contents of her stomach suddenly rose to her throat. What was she doing? This was crazy, a deadly game of roulette. But she knew they would never go through with it anyway. It was just a drunk game. She gripped the side of the counter to keep from falling. A crooked smile distorted the smooth lines of her face.

"What happens to the last envelope?" Kim asked.

"Burn it," Nicole said. "Give it here. I'll do it."

Tess tossed her the envelope. Nicole held it over the flame from the candle and they all watched the paper curl, burn, and disintegrate into ash.

"We can really do this," Kim said, as if the idea had finally come together in her mind.

"You damned right we can." Nicole polished off her drink.

Kim shifted her body. "I think it's the perfect solution to our problems," Kim said, moving into CEO mode. "There's no connection between any of us. But we must keep it that way."

"Right."

"Yeah."

"No more personal contact until after the deeds are done," Kim said.

"How will we know?" Nicole asked.

"Check the papers," Tess said simply. "Put an ad in the classified: position filled but more jobs available."

"But how do we know that any of us are really gonna do it?" Nicole looked from Kim to Tess.

"Because it's the perfect alibi. We get rid of our problem and have nothing to do with it. We don't know what name is in the envelope, so we can never tell. And no one will ever suspect a perfect stranger."

"To me, this is business," Kim said, her voice cold and indif-ferent. "I'm a businesswoman and a woman of my word. If I say I will, consider it done."

"You have my word, too," Tess said.

"My word is my bond," Nicole added.

"Let's make a toast."

The three women stood and raised their near-empty glasses.

"To getting what's ours," Tess said.

"Success," Kim tossed in.

"Retribution."

They touched glasses and emptied the contents.

"We have one last chance to walk away from it all," Tess said. "Tomorrow, arrive for your doctor's appointment as sched-uled. Whoever doesn't show up, we know is out. And it will be up to whoever shows up to follow through with the plan." Kim and Nicole nodded. "No talking, no meeting. No one must ever put us together."

CHAPTER FOUR

LIVING A LIE

Tess sat naked on the used couch in her living room and surfed through the television channels, hoping to land on something that would hold her attention until it was time for her appointment. She'd slipped out of the suite just after sunrise, and was lucky enough to find a cab to take her back to her car. The power came back on around ten and the old window air conditioner started to blow lukewarm air into the room. Stretching her damp body along the length of the couch, her gaze drifted toward the opened white envelope on the table. Muted images of the night before played in front of her. The pact, the revelations. She wondered what name Nicole or Kim received. A smile gently curved her wide mouth.

She finally settled on a Jerry Springer episode when she decided to make a call. The easiest way to get an inside scoop is to find out from someone inside.

"Hello?"

"Hey, Tracy. It's me, Tess."

"Hello, Tess. I hope you're not calling to tell me you're in

some exotic country again. And how with my job I'll never go
any further than the top floor of the court building."

"And how are you today, Tracy?" Tess asked, instead of ris-
ing to the ever-ready bait Tracy always dangled in front of her.

"I'm fine, working hard. How about you?"

Tess gritted her teeth. Now was not the time to get into yet
another sparring match with her sister. It was an ongoing debate
that had no immediate end in sight. "Actually, I'm in Florida."

"I know you didn't call to give me your itinerary or to gloat
about another shopping spree in Europe. So what can I do for
you?"

Tess wanted to shake her, tell her self-righteous sister to
stop with the martyr routine. It was old and wearing on her last
nerve.

"I'm still hard-pressed to understand how you can afford it
all on a stewardess's salary."

Tess lit a cigarette and blew a cloud of smoke into the air
before answering. "I told you about investing, but you never listen to me."

Tracy ignored the barbed comment. "I need to go. I have
tickets to see *A Raisin in the Sun*."

"Have a good time."

"I will."

"I saw you on the cover of the *Daily News* yesterday." Tess
said quickly, hoping the lure would glean some information.
Tracy always softened her hard stance if there was any room in
the conversation that praised her in some way.

"Part of the job," she said in her usual smug fashion. "But
this is going to be a big case. I can feel it. It might be the case
that will make my career."

Tess's stomach knotted as she heard the ring of pride in her sister's voice. Tracy's success would mean Tess's downfall. The most troubling question for Tess was: Would it matter to Tracy if she discovered the woman she was searching for was her own sister? For twins, they were as different as the sun and the moon. Perhaps that was because they were fraternal instead of identical, Tess always reasoned. Together, they looked related—but apart, no one would ever make the connection, which was fine with Tess. Tracy fought for truth and justice and lived her life by the letter of the law. Tess, on the other hand, considered those values an encumbrance in her line of work, and took immense pride in doing what she did so well.

"This is probably the biggest vice bust since the Mayflower Madam case," Tracy was saying. "If I can nail Madam X, I can write my own ticket. It's only a matter of time."

Tess took a chance. "Any leads?"

"We're working on it. I really can't talk to you about this. I know you understand."

"Sure. Just askin'. Anyway, uh, you enjoy yourself."

"Thanks. Where did you say you were?" she asked, easily slipping into her ADA role.

"Florida," she said, without hesitation. "I, uh . . . caught the news about the blackout. Is everything okay?"

"It was a little crazy for a while. Fortunately, I was off yesterday and didn't get stuck in all that mayhem. Other than some defrosted food, everything is fine."

"Good. Well, I'm flying to California in the morning."

"Safe travels."

"Yeah, thanks." Tess pressed the phone icon and disconnected the call. She leaned her head back against the cushion.

Most days the strained relationship between her and Tracy was no more than a blip on the radar screen. She'd blow off Tracy's snide remarks and digs at her character.

If Tracy ever discovered that her "darling" twin sister was the highest paid, most successful madam on the East Coast in the past forty years, it might kill her, but she'd rise from the grave just to snap the cuffs on and pose for photos.

The relentless feud between the sisters was as natural for them as breathing. For longer than Tess cared to remember, she and Tracy had been on opposing sides, from looks to attitude. Tracy was a nearly flawless beauty, while Tess worked at looking good. But Tracy, though naturally appealing to the eye, never mastered Tess's classy flair for clothes, the charismatic way she could capture a room, or her raw sensuality, traits that served Tess well.

Their parents doted on Tracy and always held her up as an example to the troublesome Tess. "Why can't you be more like your sister?" was said so often that she still heard the damning words in her sleep.

Tracy was dubbed "the good twin," by family and friends, while Tess found herself in one scrape after another. It wasn't so much that she was "bad," she simply wanted someone to pay her attention. She wanted to be *somebody*, not an "almost replica" of someone else. She had a wild and curious spirit, the total opposite of Tracy who was "the lady." Tracy didn't climb trees or steal fruit or kiss boys on the school stairwells or embarrass the entire family when she needed to get an abortion at seventeen. Tracy was the good daughter, the good student, and the good friend to everyone except her sister; a friendship that Tess secretly and desperately craved. Over time, the longing turned to resentment, then acceptance. So they moved into a cordial existence, with cursory phone calls and the required cards for all the appropriate occasions.

Tess sniffed back the hurt and the memories. Damn shame, she thought. But she couldn't dwell on what might have been. It was much too late.

Tess picked herself up from the couch. Her bare feet made *slap, slap* noises against the wood floor. Entering her bedroom, she was momentarily relieved by the fleeting breeze that gently lifted the white curtains.

She sat down on the side of the bed and peeked out the window.

Mr. Man from the other night was slowly strolling down the street looking just as polished and dangerous in the daylight.

Did he have a sixth sense, or the ability of a wolf to sniff out his prey? Tess wasn't sure which, but he glanced straight up at her window as if he knew she was sitting there naked as a jaybird looking at him. She swore she saw the sun flash against the white of his smile. Quickly, she dropped the curtain and ducked out of the frame of the window.

As she sat on the edge of the bed, unmoving, like a deer trapped in the headlights, she realized her heart was pounding. She dared to take a peek. He was nowhere to be seen. Poof; gone like she'd only imagined him staring up at her.

Shaking her head, she sprung up and crossed the room to snatch her robe from the hook on the back of the closet door.

It wasn't that she was ashamed of her body. If anything, she was acutely proud of it. Her body is what earned her her living and notoriety. At the age of forty, she knew she could easily give a fever to many of the twenty-somethings who swore they had it going on. Sure, gravity tried to lay claim to a few parts here and there. But it gave her womanly frame character and a little nip and tuck from time to time didn't hurt either.

She parted the folds of her robe and stood in front of the mirror. Her waist still had a nice curve to it, and the C-cup breasts held just the right amount of fullness and lift and they were all hers. Her gaze traveled downward to the dark, thick patch between her toned thighs. Locked in there was her box of gold, her "talking box." With a few quick pulls from her inner walls, she'd been known to make grown men holler for their mothers, speak in tongues, promise her the world, and whisper secrets in her ear that no one should hear except them and their Maker.

She didn't "entertain" as much as she once did. She had her favorite one or two that she would share a night with just to stay on the top of her game. But the others, men who would frequent her establishment, were just as content to share her time, tell her their troubles, or simply reminisce about how good that "last time" was between them.

No, it definitely wasn't that she was trying to hide her nakedness. It was just . . . she didn't know what it was, she realized with growing annoyance. There was simply something about that man that rubbed her the wrong way.

Tess pushed out a sigh and fastened the belt on her robe. She rifled through the few belongings in the closet that she was able to grab in a hurry and take with her—mostly designer suits, nothing remotely appropriate for the weather. Finally, she located a sundress in a soft peach color with covered buttons down the front. She pulled it from the closet.

"When was the last time I wore this old thing?" She held it up in front of her and walked to the mirror that sat on top of the used dresser. "Sometimes you just have to make do."

She wondered if Kim and Nicole would show up.

CHAPTER FIVE
FORMING ALLIANCES

Kimberly dressed quickly. She'd gotten in from the hotel barely an hour earlier, but she wanted to be out of the house and long gone before Troy got up. The nerve, she fumed as she applied her mascara—serving her divorce papers but refusing to move out! Every time she thought about the gall of the man, she was tempted to suffocate him in his sleep. Now, there was someone to do it for her.

Thank goodness their Long Island estate was big enough for the two of them. With careful planning and timing they'd never have to see each other. Their communication had been reduced to phone calls from their respective attorneys or messages via the housekeeper.

Kimberly faced her reflection in the mirror. There was a new laugh line on the right corner of her mouth, she noticed, lightly touching the imperfection. How it got there was a mystery. She couldn't remember the last time she laughed with any real sincerity.

Her days consisted of running her empire: the magazine, the

home product line, and her weekly television show. One didn't reach her level of success in the business world with smiles, especially if one was a woman. You had to be cold, calculating, and ruthless. You had to grow balls and be ready to play with them in a man's world. The only mistake she'd made on her rise up the corporate ladder of success was marrying Troy Benning.

The lazy S.O.B. was gorgeous to look at, excellent in bed, and gave validation of her womanness to the world, ultimately taking the spotlight off her other life—her real love. Troy was attentive and loving in public, and photographed like a cover model. To the fawning paparazzi, they were the golden couple.

She slammed the hairbrush down on the dressing tabletop with such force it snapped in half. Her blue eyes darkened as they filled with burning tears of fury. Hot color rose to her cheeks. How could she have been so stupid, so careless? She'd gotten complacent and took her relationship with Stephanie as a right and now it might cost them both.

Whatever she needed to do to keep what she had, she would do, no matter what. She didn't get to where she was in life by giving up and giving in. She thought about the pact, the white envelope in her jacket pocket. It had plagued her in her dreams, the name, printed in a shaky script taunted her. Was she willing to do what it took?

Kimberly straightened, checked her makeup, then smoothed the front of her butter yellow suit jacket and stood. She'd find a way, a plan. She always did. She picked up her purse and walked out.

CHAPTER SIX
PROCEED WITH CAUTION

Nicole awoke with her bra and panties sticking to her body. She slowly opened her eyes and squinted against the sun beaming in through the living room window. She glanced around and tried to get her bearings. Sounds of activity filtered through her head and it took her a moment to realize where she was. It was only the second day in eighteen months that she hadn't been awakened at 6 A.M. and herded to the shower with the other inmates. Her head pounded. She yawned and rubbed her eyes. What a day, what a night, she thought as the previous day's events slowly began to unfurl.

Images of Tess and Kim and being trapped in that metal box flashed in her head. She could still feel the sense of dread that seized her in the elevator. She glanced at the chipped coffee table. The unopened envelope was still there. And then the conversation of the night before began to replay. Slowly, she reached for the envelope, tore it open, and stared at the sheet of paper. Her pulse raced. She studied the name, and pieced to-

gether everything that had been said about the mark. She tore
the name and the envelope into tiny pieces, dropped them in
the ashtray, and burned them.

It had taken her nearly two hours to get home on the trains
once they started running. She'd tiptoed in around eleven to a
silent house and crashed on the couch.

She peeled herself off the make-believe-leather couch and
stumbled into the kitchen. Her brother Ricky was at the stove
fixing eggs.

"Morning," she muttered, then yawned loudly.

Ricky glanced over his shoulder and quickly turned away.
"Put on some clothes, Nikki."

She looked down at her seminude body. "Too hot to sleep in
clothes."

"You ain't sleeping now and I don't want you walking
around here like that."

Nicole started to tell him that even in lockup they had air-
conditioning, and if he had some she wouldn't have to sleep
"like that," but she thought better.

"When did you get in? Where did you sleep last night? I was
worried."

He would never understand that she wound up sleeping in a
hotel room with some big society white chick who wanted to
kill her husband and a high-priced hooker determined to get her
business back.

"The lights went out right in the doc's office. I crashed there
on a couch till morning. Finally made it in when the trains
started running again. Are you working today?"

"Going to meet a client. I'm putting in a new kitchen for

them. But they keep changing their minds about what they want."

"How is business?"

Her brother ran a small, not very profitable, home improvement business. Since they were kids, he'd always been good with his hands. He was forever fixing stuff and taking things apart. He didn't make a lot of money, since most of his clients didn't have much, but he made ends meet doing odd jobs in between. He'd taken care of her and her four sisters since their parents died and he had to drop out of school at sixteen.

Ricky shrugged. "Business is so-so. Could be better, but it could be worse."

Nicole shook her head. That was her *hijo*, always the optimist, seeing pies in the skies. There'd been times when all six of them had to share one big bowl of rice and beans. But Ricky never complained. He'd convince them that things were going to get better.

When Nicole saw how hard her brother worked and how tired he was, she knew she had to do something. She never told him the things the landlord made her do with him and his friends to let them stay. Then one day, hanging out on One-Hundred-and-Sixteenth Street, her friend introduced her to Trust and her life had not been the same since.

"If you're hungry I'll fix you a plate. Julia is still asleep. They canceled her classes today." Julia was the baby of the family and devoted to Nicole and Ricky. Nicole's older sister, Petra, was stabbed to death by her husband years earlier. Carmen, her next sister, left home nearly six years earlier and never returned, and Nina, the sister between Nicole and Julia, married some guy named Joel Bernstein and lived on Long Island. She never came to visit the old neighborhood. But she did call around the holidays every couple of years.

Nicole knew how deeply the family situation hurt Ricky. He'd tried so hard. That's why it was so important to her that she find a way to make his life easier.

Ricky lifted several strips of bacon from the pan and laid them on a paper towel. "I'm gonna have to throw some of this stuff out if we don't cook it up tonight. Everything in the freezer defrosted. Maybe we can ask cousin Lila and Millicent to come by later. Have a real family dinner."

Nichole pushed up from the chair, walked up behind her brother, and placed her hand on his back. "I love you, bro."

He turned halfway to look at her and smiled. When he did that his eyes lit up and it made her smile inside.

"Don't worry about me for breakfast. I'm gonna take a shower, wash some of this sweat off. Then I have to go out. The doc rescheduled my appointment. But I'll be sure to get home early and start cooking. Okay?"

She walked out of the tiny kitchen with the peeling wallpaper and into the equally small bathroom with the dripping sink. She watched the water make its methodical descent into the stained bowl. Kim Sheppard didn't live like this and she'd bet money that Tess didn't either. She wanted what they had. She wanted a decent place to live, nice clothes, a car that wasn't stolen, and money in the bank. She wanted to pay her brother back for all his sacrifices.

Nicole stepped under the beat of the cool water and let it splash over her face and down her body. Yeah, she would be there this afternoon. She knew she had heart. If she could pull off some of the stuff she'd done for Trust without a blink, there wasn't much that could scare her. The memories of uncaring hands, mouths, and things she didn't want to remember on and in her body fueled the rage within her. The rush of adrenalin made her limbs tingle with anticipation. She smiled.

CHAPTER SEVEN

DECISIONS

Dr. Hutchinson turned toward the door of the exam room. She smiled as she pushed aside the cart containing her tools of the trade. "Good to see you, as always, Tess. What a mess yesterday, huh? What did you do?"

"Stayed with a friend."

"You were lucky. I got stuck in traffic on the way to delivering a baby. Suffice it to say that baby arrived long before I did."

They laughed.

"Okay, you know the drill. Hop up on the table and spread 'em." She chuckled.

"Your stirrup-side manner hasn't improved much, Annette."

"Hard to teach an old dog new tricks. *Some* old dogs, anyway." She winked at Tess and snapped on a pair of latex gloves, then adjusted the standing light for a better view. "How have you been?"

"Not as well as I would like, to be honest."

"I read the article in the *Daily News*." She pressed down on Tess's abdomen as she adjusted the speculum. "What are you going to do?"

There were maybe three people in the world that Tess trusted with her secret—Annette Hutchinson was one of them. They'd met years ago at a medical shindig when Tess was in the market for a good doctor who was also discreet. Tess was the escort for one of the doctors—a surgeon who was also one of her regular clients.

Annette had approached their table during a break from one of the endless speeches to say hello to her colleague.

"John, my goodness, how long has it been?"

John stood, a broad smile on his face. He extended his arms and kissed both of her cheeks.

"Annette, beautiful as always. How have you been?"

"Busy and busier." She laughed a rich, no-holds-barred laugh and Tess immediately liked her.

John turned to his date. "Tess McDonald, this is Dr. Annette Hutchinson."

Tess extended her hand. "Nice to meet you. What is your specialty?"

"OB-GYN."

"Really? Where do you practice?"

"I have an office in downtown Manhattan." She reached into her purse and pulled her business card out of a gold case. "Call if you ever need me." She smiled, displaying a perfect set of dimples in her nut brown face.

Tess took the card. "I certainly will." And she did.

About two weeks later, Tess made her first appointment, then went back several times in the following months to get a feel for Annette.

They were sitting in Annette's office after Tess's exam when Annette finally broached the question that had been bubbling inside her for months. She slipped off her glasses and looked directly into Tess's unwavering eyes.

"You've been in here to see me six times in as many months. Other than a minor yeast infection, there's nothing wrong with you." She leaned forward, her forearms braced on the desktop. "I can tell, however, that you engage in an extremely active sex life." She paused a beat as she watched the array of expressions move across Tess's face—from surprise to amusement. "What do you do for a living, Tess?"

Tess crossed her long legs and folded her hands in her lap. She lifted her chin by a notch and a wicked smile matched the look in her eyes. "I make men happy."

There was an instant of shock that quickly shifted to acceptance of what she'd long suspected. "I see." She closed the folder on her desk. "Are you good at it?"

Tess tossed her head back and laughed—a mixture of relief and merriment. "So I've been told."

That was the beginning of a friendship that had lasted more than ten years, and in all that time Annette had never treated her any differently than any other patient.

"What am I going to do?" Tess said, absently repeating Annette's question. "Right now, I'm not really sure," she lied with ease. "I've had to leave my apartment—which I can't tell you how much I miss. I was barely able to take anything with me, and I'm staying in Brooklyn, of all places."

"You, in Brooklyn!" She chuckled.

"I know. I say the same thing every morning when I look out the window." She got down from the table and proceeded to get dressed.

"At some point, Tess, you're going to have to make some decisions about the rest of your life. What about the others?"

The twenty women who'd been part of Tess's booming enterprise were all patients of Annette. But Tess knew that her question was not out of concern for her practice but a deep concern for the women whom she'd come to know.

Tess sighed. "After I got the tip I sent everyone packing. They're all gone, all over the place." She buttoned her dress.

"Maybe it's time you give this life up."

"Please, Nettie, don't lecture me. I know where you're heading." She dropped her arms to her sides. "It may not be an honorable profession I'm in, but I never hurt anyone, I never stole, cheated, or lied. All I've done is use what I was born with to make men happy—and myself a wealthy woman. I've traveled, and met some of the most incredible people. I simply make men pay for what other women give away willingly.

"And someone thinks they have the right to take that away from me! Why? Because I've committed some great sin?" She stepped into her open-backed shoes.

"For God's sakes Tess, let it go. You've had a good run. Walk away while you still can."

Tess turned away. "I don't think so, Annette."

Annette opened her mouth, but nothing came out.

Tess picked up her purse from the desk. "Thank you for being my friend, Nettie." She leaned forward and kissed Annette's cheek. "And don't worry, I'll be fine."

Annette watched in silence as Tess walked out, and wondered if the next time she saw Tess it would be as her patient or on the late-night news. In all the years she'd known and come to admire Tess McDonald, and listened to her share her exploits in the confines of the small office, this was the first time Annette was actually afraid for her friend.

Tess walked out into the waiting room. She tucked her clutch purse beneath her arm and looked around. Five women sat in various sections of the inviting space—reading magazines, watching the infomercial, or rubbing rounded bellies. None of them were Kim or Nicole.

The weight of disappointment was sudden, surprising Tess as it dropped into the pit of her stomach. She'd been so sure. She checked her watch. It was nearly three. If they were coming they would have been there already. Resigned, she left and walked to the elevator, where less than twenty-four hours earlier, three perfect strangers dared to crack open the door to their inner demons and reveal their dark secrets.

She lowered her head. "It was just a story."

The elevator door slid open and Tess looked up and into the faces of Nicole and Kim. The weight in her stomach slowly eased as a half smile tugged at her mouth.

Tess entered the elevator. Kim walked into the waiting area. Nikki went to the ladies room.

The elevator door slid shut.

And so it begins, she thought.

CHAPTER EIGHT

MAKING MOVES

Tess parked her used Toyota Camry a half block away from her building and walked the short distance down the street, weaving her way around the cyclists, dog walkers, racing kids, and car-sitters that peppered the street.

She'd stashed her Lexus in the private garage uptown and paid for two months in advance. Hopefully in that time all this mess would be straightened out—whatever that meant. She certainly hoped that Kim and Nicole had what it was going to take to pull the plan off. Nicole certainly had the passion and the fearlessness, but her hot temper could pose a problem if she wasn't watched. She was driven by pure emotion—a dangerous fuel. Kim, on the other hand, was just as volatile but in a refined sense. She was methodical, and as driven as both she and Nicole, but Kim hid it behind a veneer of upper-crust privilege. They'd set off on a long and dangerous road, and there was no room for their shortcomings.

The rancid scent of garbage sitting in the heat for too long wafted on the heavy air like cheap perfume. She hoped she'd remembered to close her windows or her tiny apartment would smell like a sewer for hours.

"Good evening, pretty lady."

The sound of the now-familiar baritone voice reached out to her from behind the shade of the tree. Tess turned and the body took shape in the night. She forced herself to focus on his eyes, and not the rippling muscles that glistened in the dark and longed to burst from the cropped white T-shirt set against the milk chocolate of his skin.

"Hello," she murmured.

A heartbreaking grin broke out across his wide mouth, exposing those pearly whites that had gleamed up at her from the street when she'd spotted him from her window.

"Ahh, the lady speaks." He folded his arms and leaned against a black BMW as his eyes searched every inch of her body.

Tess thought she was still walking, but realized she'd come to a complete stop. She swallowed hard. He was young and dangerous, she concluded. Sex rolled off him like heat snakes ready to wrap around any unsuspecting victim. It wouldn't be her.

"I speak when I need to," she tossed back, suddenly feeling like playing the baiting game. Her brow arched in challenge.

He didn't move but continued to stare at her with that smile that wouldn't let her feet leave the spot.

"Hot, huh?" His lids lowered, shielding his eyes.

"Generally is this time of year."

He lifted his chin. "How about you and me sharing an ice cold beer to take the heat off?"

Tess angled her head to the side. "You're kidding me, right?"

"Nope." He puckered his lips. "As a matter of fact, I have your brand in a cooler in the trunk. Coors, right?"

All pretenses of fronting drifted off with the rank air as Tess cracked up laughing. "You are a real piece of work. Do you generally lounge around waiting for women to walk by so that you can offer them a beer?"

"Hmmm, not generally. But you have to admit, the offer is intriguing." He grinned and a hot tingle spread between her thighs. "So what do you say? Nothing fancy. We could sit right here or up there on your stoop."

"Give me a good reason why I should and maybe I'll think about it."

He pushed himself up off the car and she realized for the first time how tall he was. She was compelled to look up into his eyes.

He shrugged slightly and lowered his head to look directly into her eyes. "Cause the truth is, I don't usually do this. So that means you must be someone special and I want to check that out for myself."

Tess tugged in a short, quick breath, intoxicated by the clean soap and water scent of him even in all the heat.

"How can a girl resist being considered 'possibly' special?"

He chuckled. "I'll be here." He leaned back against the car. "No pressure."

Tess gave him one long look then continued the few short steps to the front of her building before she realized that her knees felt wobbly. *Damn.*

Tess practically ran up the stairs, once she'd gotten the door closed and locked behind her, feeling like he might be hot on her heels and if he was—well she wasn't certain what she might do.

Once inside her apartment she allowed herself a moment to catch her breath, clear her head, and analyze what the hell just happened out there.

She kicked off one shoe, then the other, picked them up, and went into her bedroom. What was wrong with her? She was a professional, for heaven's sake. She had men for breakfast, lunch, dinner, and snacks, and never batted an eye or allowed herself to remotely feel anything for any of them. It was a job, nothing more. The last time she'd allowed herself the luxury of feeling anything for a man, other than for the size of his wallet, or an occasional bout of lust, she'd paid dearly for it.

It still hurt, all these years later, she realized as she slipped out of her dress. Since then she'd hidden her emotions behind a wall of feigned indifference, cool calculations, and detachment. It was the only way she survived. In her line of work there was no room for emotional attachments. That only bred trouble. But how many nights had she lain in the arms of some man wishing for something more than for it to be over?

Sure, she'd had fun along the way, met incredible people, laughed, traveled, and wallowed in gifts and accolades. Over time she'd moved away from the "work" of the job to simply being the consummate hostess and keen businesswoman. In the process, she'd missed a great deal. Most times she didn't think about it, but tonight—tonight she did. She glanced toward the open window, listened to the sounds of Teddy Pendergrass's *You Got What I Need* blasting from the speakers of a passing car, and wondered if the sexy stranger had what she needed—if only for one night.

CHAPTER NINE

PRIVATE AGENDA

Kim pulled up in front of her estate. The lights in the east wing were blazing. Frustration clamped her jaw in a viselike grip. Troy didn't pay a damned dime for the upkeep of the house, but he had no qualms about availing himself of its amenities.

She turned the key only halfway in the ignition, opting to sit a few more minutes in the car to get her temper under control. She leaned back against the leather headrest and closed her eyes while the newscaster droned on about the usual events of the day: terror alerts, a recap of the blackout, subway shootings, and the standard celebrity scandal. It wasn't until the voice took a breath for a special announcement that Kim really sat up and paid attention.

"Incumbent Senator Malcolm Abrams has successfully won the Republican nomination against contender Nick Davis. Abrams will have a hard fight for the seat against Democrat Horace Dukes, who has built an impressive following in the past six months of campaigning."

She breathed deeply. This day was bound to arrive. Now it

was more important than ever to ensure that her husband never uttered a word to anyone.

She reached for her cell phone and punched in the code for Stephanie's private line. On the third ring, Stephanie picked up.

"Hi. It's me."

Stephanie turned in a small circle in the control room to make sure no one was nearby. "I was hoping you'd call. I was worried."

"I just heard the news on the radio about Malcolm."

"Yes."

Kim could hear the smile of pride in her voice and wondered how Stephanie could so easily manipulate her emotions and her allegiances. There were times when Stephanie spoke about Malcolm as if he was the greatest, most important person in her life, even as she lay in bed with Kim. And it made her wonder if the secret life that she and Stephanie shared was no more than an experiment for Stephanie.

"I found out earlier today. But we were pretty certain for weeks that Mal would get the nod. I guess we'll be on the campaign trail in the next few weeks."

"I know. That's what I need to talk to you about, what I wanted to talk to you about the other night."

"What is it? You sound . . . you don't sound like yourself."

Kim glanced up at her house. "Can you meet me tomorrow at The Grill?"

"Tomorrow is going to be crazy. Reporters are crawling all over us already. I doubt if I can get away. Tell me what it is."

Kim shut her eyes for a moment. "Troy knows." She held her breath as she waited for the words to sink in with Stephanie.

"What?" A knot twisted so tight inside her stomach it

forced her voice to come out in a hiss. "What are you talking about—he knows?"

"Everything about us. He filed for divorce and has threatened to go to the press if I don't turn over my company and my assets to him as part of the settlement."

Bile rose to Stephanie's throat, accompanied by a body heat that made her feel momentarily faint. She breathed deeply then slowly sat down. Another wave of nausea rolled through her stomach.

"I don't understand," she said, speaking as if the language were new to her and untried. "What are we going to do?" Her hands shook when she envisioned the ramifications: the look on Malcolm's face when he found out, the headlines, the gossip. She might be able to weather the storm, but Malcolm would be ruined. He didn't deserve that and she would not allow it to happen. "Then you give him what he wants," she said, her tone deathly calm.

"What! You can't mean that."

Stephanie's green eyes narrowed. "Like hell I don't. Give him what he wants, Kim. I mean it. I won't have that sonofabitch ruin my life and Mal's."

"What about my life?"

"You should have thought about that before you let him find out."

"Steph."

The call disconnected.

Kim dialed the number again and the call went directly to Stephanie's voicemail. She waited a few minutes and tried again. Voicemail.

Her throat burned as her eyes filled with hot tears. She

pressed a fist to her mouth to hold back the sob that pushed against her lips.

Stephanie couldn't mean it, she reasoned. She was stunned, upset. Of course she didn't expect Kim to give up everything to appease Troy. That was not the Stephanie she knew. She shook her head. It was the shock, that's all. Stephanie loved her. She wouldn't want to see her hurt and left with nothing.

Kim sniffed back her tears. She'd give Stephanie a couple of days to think about it and then she'd call back and explain. Everything would be fine. It had to be.

Troy. He was not going to take her business and she would not let him take Stephanie from her either. Whatever needed to be done to keep what was hers, she was willing to do. The name inside the envelope flashed in front of her.

She turned off the car and got out. Whatever doubts or inhibitions she may have harbored vanished. As her heels popped against the concrete path to the front door, her resolve grew with every step.

Reluctant, but determined, Kim went inside, closing the door gently behind her. She stood for a moment in the foyer listening for sounds of life. Phyllis suddenly appeared, as if mentally summoned.

"Good evening, Mrs. Benning. Dinner is all prepared."

"Thank you. Where is Mr. Benning?"

"In the solarium."

Kim proceeded down the foyer to the sitting room, picking up the mail from the hall table en route. She made a show of looking at her watch. "Why don't you go on home, Phyllis. I'm sure we won't be needing anything else tonight."

"Yes, ma'am."

"As a matter of fact, why don't you take tomorrow off?" She swung toward Phyllis in time to catch the look of surprise on her face.

"But tomorrow isn't my regular day off."

Kim smiled. "Don't worry about it. You'll still get your full pay." She paused and looked Phyllis in the eye. "You could use a day to do something for yourself for a change. Spend some time with your family."

"If you're sure," she finally said.

Kim's practiced smile never faltered. "Quite. Have a good evening." She turned away and began opening the mail.

Once she heard Phyllis's car pull out of the driveway, she went directly to her bedroom to prepare.

CHAPTER TEN

BEST SERVED COLD

The atmosphere was palpable on One-Hundred-and-Sixteenth Street. The air was filled with the scents of weed, cigarettes, perfume, fried fish, and plantains.

Nicole catwalked down the street, checking out all the old hangout spots and seeing who was still representing on the corners. Her veins became infused with the energy, the sultry romanticism of the street, like an addict filling up on her drug of choice. This was her world, a place where she felt comfortable, accepted, respected. She lifted her chin, tossing her mane of hair across her shoulder, even as some of the new chicas on the block threw dirty looks as she passed. They would know who she was soon enough, she thought. She cut her eyes in their direction, daring them with a look to speak up. That's when she heard one of them say, "That's Trust's woman. She's back."

Nicole's mouth formed a smug smile and her hips swayed just a bit harder. Yeah, she was back, so step off, her looks and her attitude screamed.

"Yo, Nikki."

She turned her head toward the sound of her name and damn if her heart didn't jump out of her pocket and settle in her throat. Standing next to her running buddy Monroe was Trust.

Nicole lifted her chin in acknowledgment and forced herself to breathe.

Monroe sauntered over to her and kissed her cheek. "How you been girl? Looking good, as always." His eyes ran up and down her lush body with a hunger that belied his casual words. "They treat you awright in there?"

She stepped back and twisted her mouth. Her stance and expression grew hard. "Whadda you care? Don't recall seeing *your* name on the visitors' list." Her nostrils flared in contempt even as she snatched a look at Trust, who had yet to budge from his lean against a silver Mercedes. *New*, Nicole thought absently.

"Aw come on, Nik, don't be like that. You know we glad to have you back. Couldn't risk comin' up there. You know that."

Nicole rolled her eyes.

Monroe put his arm around her stiff shoulders. "Come on and say hello." He urged her toward Trust.

She felt like digging her heels into the concrete and making Monroe drag her over there, but she didn't want to cause a scene.

On stiff legs, she approached.

His hooded eyes took her in. Women thought that look was sexy and dreamy, but Nicole knew better. Trust was flying high.

"Hey, baby," he crooned. A slow smile moved across his mouth for an instant and a rim of gold flashed.

Nicole stepped up to him. "Trust."

"You could sound more enthusiastic. That's how you say hello to your man after all this time?"

"Shouldn't have been *all this time*."

His arm lassoed around her waist and pulled her full against him. He looked down at her and brushed her lips with his thumb. "I missed you. You know that Nik."

"How do I know?" she asked and wished she hadn't sounded like she was begging.

He pressed closer, held her tighter. She felt the bulge push between her legs and knew even as she hated what he'd allowed to happen to her, she still ached for him. Her one weakness and he knew it.

Nicole pulled away. "I have to go." The stunned look on his face was worth the denial her body was going through.

He jutted his chin, then gave a short nod. "It's like that, huh?"

Nicole leaned back on her legs and braced her right hand on her hip. "You tell me what it's like, Trust, see, 'cause I been outta the loop for a minute."

"You know that's how it had to go down. If I woulda taken the fall the judge would still be counting the years. Naw, couldn't let that happen."

"What about me? You ever give a damn about what happened to me in there?"

Trust's eyes darted left then right to see who had stopped doing what they were doing to listen. He wasn't about to let Nik dis him in the street. Not in front of his people. He grabbed her arm and hustled her inside his car before she had a chance to react.

Behind the tinted windows he turned to her, his eyes cloaked and dangerous. The gold incisor flashed inside the dim interior.

"Look, you knew the deal going in. This ain't no game. This is business—*my* business." He pounded on his chest for emphasis. "And I can't conduct it if they got me on lockdown." He looked her over, and seeing the unchanged, disinterested expression on her face, he knew that his monologue hadn't moved her, so he changed tactics and tone. "You think I wanted to see you go down?" He licked his lips. "I love you, girl. You know that." Her reached out and stroked the back of her neck. Her eyes fluttered along with her heart. "Come 'ere." His command was thick and seductive.

Nicole felt so weak—as if her mind and body were no longer of use to her. His hand found her thigh and moved possessively along the tender inside. She fought back the tremor that ran the length of her body.

Trust applied a bit more pressure, his free hand seeking the rise of her breasts that practically spilled from her top. He lifted the weight in his palm.

A soft hiss blew through her lips.

"That's my girl." His other hand eased up her thigh until he found what he was hunting for. "You know I missed you." His hand cupped her and squeezed. He leaned in and kissed her cheek, then her ear.

"Not like . . . this," she managed to say, twisting away from his grasp.

Trust jerked back. "What's with you?" His expression turned malevolent. Deep furrows etched themselves in his brow and the corners of his mouth.

She'd practiced the words a hundred times since earlier that afternoon. All she had to do now was say them—open her mouth and say them.

Nicole tentatively reached out to caress his cheek. He pulled away, his dark eyes stabbing her as sharply as a pointed blade.

"Come on, baby, it's been too long for our first time together to be all squeezed up in a car. I'm supposed to be your woman, right?"

"Yeah . . . supposed to be."

"So then we need to celebrate my homecoming, right?" She pressed against him, letting her breasts brush his bare arm.

Temptation lifted the corner of his mouth as his expression smoothed out like a wrinkled shirt treated to a hot iron and some starch.

"Awright, so let's go to my place."

Nicole reached for the door handle and unlocked it. "For once, we're gonna do things my way, on my time." She laughed as her hand rubbed the bulge in his pants, then gently massaged it. She blew him a kiss and got out, knowing that in the condition she left him in, he wasn't up to following her.

She stepped from the car and with a slick smile of triumph on her lips, she continued down the block toward home. She stopped for a second in front of the trio of women on the corner. "You were right—I'm back." She winked and walked off.

CHAPTER ELEVEN

NO WAY OUT

Trust sat within the dim confines of his ride; the hum of the air conditioner was the only sound as he tossed around in his head what had just gone down between him and Nicole. She looked the same, sounded and smelled the same, but she was a different chick from the one he knew eighteen months earlier. He understood all too well what time behind bars could do to you.

The system tricked society into believing that jail was a place for offenders to learn a lesson and get rehabilitated so that they could come out and become a contributing member of the rat race. That was bullshit.

The joint taught you how to be a better criminal, how to angle so you wouldn't get caught next time. Learning how to wash and sort laundry wasn't like learning a skill that employers were tripping over themselves to hire you for. So, instead, before you got out, you learned better street skills, got more street contacts, and developed a burning desire never to go back inside.

Combine those things together and you wound up with

Trust Lang, a dedicated hustler who would rather sell his mama
than go back to the joint.

Trust cracked his knuckles, an unfortunate habit he'd picked
up from watching his father—just before he'd begin his weekly
ritual of beating Trust's mother on Friday nights. It was a routine
that he and his younger sister, Hope, had endured for years—at
least until Trust turned fourteen. That's when things changed.
He met Fetch, the most notorious, most feared hustler in Harlem.

At first it was small things: running packages across town or
standing outside of an establishment if Fetch's boys had to "take
care" of somebody inside. Sometimes it was escorting ladies
home after a long night at one of Fetch's Harlem bars. But, by
the time he was sixteen, he was carrying a gun. He sat in on the
plans to rob, maim, intimidate, or process a sale. He was making
anywhere from fifteen to two grand a week by the time he was
seventeen. By eighteen he was Fetch's right hand. Fetch did
nothing without Trust knowing. On the street, Trust was given
much respect, either from fear or admiration. It didn't much
matter to Trust one way or the other as long as he got his due.

By the time he was twenty, he'd done his first bid in Rikers
Island Correctional Facility, and he swore he would never go
back. He moved his mother into a two-story, four-bedroom
house on Long Island. He'd paid for his sister to go to a private
high school and had paid off the first two years of her college tu-
ition at Howard University. He'd refurbished a four-story
brownstone on One-Hundred-and-Twenty-seventh Street in
Harlem, where he lived alone, and on his twenty-first birthday
Fetch gave him the keys to an onyx 2000 Escalade with all the
trimmings, along with his own crew.

"Happy birthday, son," Fetch said, as he toasted Trust with a glass of champagne, in a room that sparkled with people dressed to impress themselves and each other. About one hundred people filled the grand ballroom of Fetch's Mt. Vernon estate.

Fetch turned to the guests. "Today is Trust's twenty-first birthday. He has been more of a son to me than anyone could that was flesh and blood. I trust him with my life and my business." He put his large hand on Trust's shoulder. "He has my authority and my protection in everything that he does. So tonight, in honor of this occasion, Trust will now be in charge of all my operations."

Trust tried to be cool, keep the shock from registering on his face and the tears out of his eyes. He pressed his lips tightly together as he looked at Fetch with disbelief.

Fetch nodded his head. "You earned it, son, from the day I told you your Friday night troubles were over," he said in a measured tone that was only meant for Trust's ears.

"To Trust!" Fetch raised his glass and all the guests followed suit.

Not more than two months later, Fetch was dead. Heart attack, the doctor said, took him in his sleep. It was then that Trust fully grasped the enormity of the enterprise that Fetch established. But he had been taught by the master, and he ran the operations and the crew with the same smooth bravado and lethal charm as his teacher.

Of all of Fetch's businesses, Trust had a passion for the cars that wound up in his chop shop, which was how he met Nicole. He was totally turned on—not only by the sexy, compact body, but by her love for cars and her innate knowledge about the design and make-up of every model.

He'd met her at one of the bars when she'd come up to him and told him she wanted to work with him. After he'd gotten over the shock of her bold introduction, they got to talking and she told him what she knew about cars. Totally out of character for him, he brought her to one of the shops and let her work on a late model Mustang they'd recently acquired. In less than six hours, she replaced the engine, filed down the VIN imprint, changed the tires, and began to repaint the body.

Even his crew had to stand back and applaud. Nicole was officially inducted into the family and duly respected as Trust's woman.

Nicole. Trust adjusted himself in the seat to relieve the pressure she'd left behind. All that stuff he'd said to her he meant. Other than his sister, Nicole was the only person he had any kind of feelings for. He hadn't wanted her to do the time, but what choice did he have? He knew she understood that.

He dug in the glove compartment and pulled out a box of Newports, lit one and took a long thoughtful drag.

Yeah, he knew what they had before she did the time, but he knew how jail could change you. How it had changed Nicole—time would tell. But she bore watching. Close watching. He checked under the seat for his piece. And, if he didn't like what he saw, he would simply make it disappear. Because feelings never stopped him from doing whatever was necessary.

CHAPTER TWELVE

DECISIONS

Tess paced across the hardwood floor—that could definitely use a good polishing, she absently observed—as she contemplated the idea of going back out to see that boy. She tugged on her bottom lip with her teeth. Yeah, a boy—a man-child—who had enough sex appeal and self-confidence that he'd given her—a woman who'd been around the block—a titillating moment of excitement.

The last time she'd been genuinely turned on by a man had been longer ago than she cared to recollect. Sure, she played an Oscar-worthy role of pretending to care, but that was all part of the job. •

When she took those precious moments to seduce them with accolades about their intellects, their bodies, their senses of humor, and listened and consoled or cajoled, then lay beneath or above them and convincingly whispered that they were the best lover she'd had, it was all part of the game.

She'd become so adept and jaded that she could go through the motions without a second thought. This, however, was different. She felt a shuddering thrill that she had not experienced since Charles—the one man she'd dared to have feelings for. She'd been young and naive back then, and had no real concept of her feminine powers. Things were different now. Funny, she'd begun to believe that her golden box was locked and the only keys able to open it were money and power.

With a toss of her head, she shattered the picture of what could have been, letting the fragments fall at her feet. Tess stepped over the shards and walked to the bathroom, shutting the door firmly behind her.

Finally showered, a hint of African musk oil teasing her wrists and the pulse in her throat, Tess stood in the center of the bedroom and stepped into her flip-flops. The short denim shirt and spaghetti strap T-shirt took a good seven years off her age. She smiled, catlike, as she checked her reflection.

"Not bad for an old broad." She snatched up her keys and headed downstairs.

When she stood at the top of the stoop, a hot shot of pleasure exploded in her stomach and spread like a fine liquor through her veins. He was still there—waiting.

Again, like a predator, he sensed her, eased up from his relaxed pose on his car, and turned toward her. His slow smile of appreciation, like a road map, led her right to him.

"Thought you'd changed your mind."

"No, you didn't." She smiled.

He laughed. "You're right." He raised his chin as he asked her name.

"Tess."

"Vincent."

Her expression remained even as she tried to determine why she was so drawn to him. He was a good-looking man, without question, just topping six feet by an inch or two, nut brown complexion with a razor-thin mustache that haloed full lips, and just a shadow of a beard that was etched around a strong jaw. His eyes were dark, dreamy, almost, often hidden behind partially lowered lids and long lashes.

She'd seen dozens of men like him—better looking, taller, more solid in build—so that wasn't it. It was his casual cool, his lack of concern for anything beyond the moment, the total self-containment that hinted at a raw, almost animal-like sensuality, that was as potent as a hallucinogenic. While it frightened her in its subtle intensity, she was inexorably intrigued.

"You're definitely not from around here," he said, halting her assessment an instant before her mind took it to the next level. He folded his arms across his chest.

"How can you tell?"

"Too much class. I'd say," he looked her up and down with a sweeping glance, "an uptown girl. Even though you did give me the finger the other night." The corner of his mouth curved. "An uptown girl with a downtown edge."

Tess laughed. "And what about you?"

He released a long, slow breath. "Around, here and there."

"Homeless?" she teased.

"I have a way of finding a place to lay my head."

Her right brow lifted. "Is that right? Must take work."

"That all depends."

"On what?"

"You."

A warm flush suffused her even as the seed of her sex hardened and twitched in anticipation.

Damn. When was the last time she'd been spoken to like that by a man—direct, straight to the point, no chasers? Longer than she cared to think about. And, she had to admit, although not to him, that it totally turned her on.

She leaned back on her left leg, taking him in at an angle. "You don't know me like that," she said.

"But I intend to. Unless, of course, you have some objections."

"A man with low self-esteem," she taunted, biting back a smile.

He laughed. "Good one." He paused a moment watching the laughter dance around her eyes and mouth. "How about that beer?"

"I thought you'd never ask."

Vincent eased up off the side of the car and walked around to the trunk. As promised, he had a cooler filled with ice and bottles of Coors. He took one out and handed it to her. He lifted his beer bottle in a toast. "To getting to know you like that."

Tess assessed him through partially lowered lids, her mouth flickering in a smile. "It takes skill and more than a bottle of Coors."

"Trust me, I have both . . . and then some."

The cat-and-mouse, bob-and-weave exchange of double entendres was fun, challenging her in a way that her usual suitable-for-dinner-guests conversation did not. As much as she was reluctant to admit, she was actually enjoying herself.

"So, we've already concluded that you are a lost uptown girl who somehow stumbled her way into the hood, sort of like a Dorothy in the Wizard of Oz."

Tess chuckled.

"How did you lose your way into this neck of the woods?"

She shrugged lightly. "Let's say I needed a change of scenery."

"From what? Seems like the horizon would be endless uptown. Over here is where the future begins to look a little murky."

"I suppose it depends on what you're looking for," she said, a bit more wistful than she intended.

Vincent looked at her for a moment. He took a long swallow of his beer. "Any chance that you'll find it?" he said in a husky tone that stroked the pit of her stomach.

She snatched in a short breath. "I intend to."

"I always admired women who knew their minds, and what they wanted out of life, not waiting on a man to tell them what to do or make all the decisions." He took another swallow of his beer.

"Then you're certainly a man of the new millennium. Most men want a woman to be dependent upon them—makes them feel manly," she said exaggerating *manly* with a sly grin. Tess leaned her hip against the tree and slid her glance along the length of his body. "So what do you do, Vincent, beside offer women bottles of beer from the trunk of your car?"

"I'm an independent businessman."

"Meaning?"

"Meaning that the only person I have to answer to is myself."

"I see."

"What about you?"

She smirked. "An independent businesswoman."

"I like that."

"So what is your independent business?"

"Let's say that I do favors for people."

"And they pay you for it, I assume."

"Very well." He grinned and she noticed the dimple beneath his right eye.

"What's your independent business?"

"I'll put it this way—and then we'll leave it alone—we have a lot in common."

Vincent stared at her through eyes at half-mast. "Best way to start a little something is a common ground." He took a long swallow of his beer. The next turn of the bottle finished it off. "Wanna go for a drive?" He tossed the empty bottle into a trash can a few feet away.

Tess knew no more about him than a hole in the wall. He could be the next serial killer or the greatest lay of her life. The way she was feeling in his presence, she silently prayed for the latter.

"Maybe another time when we get to know each other better."

He pressed his lips together and nodded. "Fair enough. Can I call you?"

Tess gave him her cell phone number, which he programmed into his.

"Cool if I call you tomorrow?"

"That's entirely up to you."

"I really like you," he said, folding his arms across his chest.

The corner of her mouth curved for an instant. "Good night, and thanks for the beer."

"My pleasure."

She flashed him a parting glance and walked across the street, walking that walk when you know a man's eyes are following your every move.

Vincent watched her retreat and waited until she'd closed the door behind her. He took his cell phone from the clip on his belt and punched in the number on speed dial. The call picked up on the second ring.

"I've made contact," he said into the phone, then disconnected the call.

He returned the phone to his belt clip, and looked up thoughtfully at Tess's windows as the lights came on, one by one.

He muttered a curse under his breath. It was times like these that he truly hated what he did for a living.

CHAPTER THIRTEEN

AND SO IT BEGINS

Kim entered her bedroom. Slowly, she glanced around at the picture-perfect space: the original artwork by Picasso, Gauguin, Rembrandt and the like that graced the winter white walls; the awards that filled the shelves of her antique étagère; the single Persian rug that sat regally in the center of the polished hard-wood floor.

She tossed her purse onto the cushy queen-sized bed and methodically took off one shoe and then the other, placing them in a perfect line inside her cedar closet. It had taken her years of hard work and sacrifice, she thought, as she removed her suit jacket and placed it across the back of the chaise lounge. A slow, bubbling fury rumbled in the pit of her belly when she thought about losing all that she'd created.

Her blue eyes darkened as they flashed toward the open door. How easy it would be to simply walk down the hallway, across to the other wing, ease into the solarium, and shoot Troy with the tiny, pearl-handled handgun she kept locked in her personal safe. She could always say she thought she heard an intruder. Or she could simply walk away and make it look like a break-in. No one in their right mind would ever believe that she was actually capable of anything that ugly. Not even John, no matter what she might have said. But there was always someone who would believe, some busybody who would uncover the truth, and she'd rather live in a hovel than behind bars.

No, Tess's plan was best: murder by a stranger. In a city like New York, tragic things happened every day.

Kim lifted her chin. If she could convince millions to invest in her products, her ideas, she could certainly convince Troy that she still loved him and that there was hope for their relationship. Tess's words rang in her head as she left the sanctity of her bedroom and headed for the solarium: "The mark rarely suspects the ones who are part of their agenda. . . ."

Troy looked up from the newspaper that was propped on his lap when Kim entered the space. His thin lips curled into what remotely resembled a sneer.

"Kim." The word sounded almost like a curse.

She stepped closer and pulled up a chair, then sat down.

"To what do I owe the pleasure of your company?"

"We haven't seen or spoken to each other in days." Her expression remained bland.

"The last time we did it wasn't what you would consider amicable."

"And I really don't see why it can't be."

He put the paper down and focused on her. "What are you saying? Are you agreeing to my terms?"

Her stomach knotted for a moment. "I've been doing a great deal of thinking since you presented your . . . ultimatum."

"I think my requests are only fair," he said, his tone sarcastic and condescending. "After all, I'm the injured party here."

Kim sucked in a breath. "I'm sure that you realize there is no way that I can turn over my entire enterprise to you."

He reached for the discarded newspaper and snapped it open. "Then there is really nothing to discuss."

Kim slowly rose from her seat and languidly began to unfasten the buttons on her blouse. Troy watched in rapt fascination. His Adam's apple bobbed up and down as the smooth, cool flesh of his wife's body was revealed in degrees. He would never admit it, especially to Kim, but there was no other woman who'd ever been able to turn him on and satisfy him the way Kim did. Sometimes all it took was for her to walk into a room and give him one of her heated blue stares and he'd nearly climax, barely able to contain his need until they were alone. When he'd found out about Kim and Stephanie Abrams, the combination of humiliation and rage had nearly killed him. How could she want another woman over him? Hadn't he always been a satisfying lover—inventive, willing to engage in all the freaky sex acts that came into her head? He was addicted to Kim. There was no other explanation, and she'd virtually ruined him for any other woman.

He'd tried to be with other women and invariably came away worse off than when he went in. Kim had no idea how deeply she'd hurt him—another man was one thing, but another woman? How could he ever hope to compete? So he wanted to hurt her, make her feel the same kind of pain he felt, and he knew the only way to accomplish that was to destroy the thing he knew she cared about above all else—her business. Maybe if he took that from her, she'd find her way back to him—where she belonged. But, of course, he could never tell her that—especially now when she stood in front of him, naked and exquisite, with the light from the moon outlining the perfection of her body.

"It's been a long time, Troy," she said, forcing down the bile that rose to her throat. She stepped closer.

Troy adjusted himself in his chair. She was right up on him now and he inhaled the womanly scent of her. It went straight to his head.

She reached out and stroked his cheek. Her eyes darkened to a deep blue.

He ran his hands along her hips and pulled her closer until the heart of her sex was right at his mouth. She closed her eyes and shuddered when his tongue tentatively flicked her once, twice, continuing in a slow but steady rhythm.

She didn't want to enjoy what he was doing to her, but her body betrayed her mind as she became a slave to the sensations that rippled through her, making her legs weak, her knees wobble. She cupped the back of his head and pushed him closer as she slowly rotated her pelvis in time to the laving of her pearl—that had hardened to a throbbing peak.

"Troy," she hissed through her teeth.

He kept at it, thrilled by what he knew he was making her feel, until he sensed the telltale escalation of her breathing, the grip that tightened, the unintelligible sounds that emanated from deep in her throat—until her body snapped and trembled and the sound of his name echoed among the profusion of plants that surrounded them.

As her shudders slowly began to dissipate, he stood, nibbling her tingling flesh as he did so. He unzipped his pants and stepped out of them, then pushed her back against the table until her legs straddled his sides.

He hated the power she had over him even as he became consumed by the heat within her walls. He wanted to pound into her, use his body to drive from her body the need for the other woman. He wanted her to cry out his name, as he imagined she did with her lover. He wanted the Kimberly that he'd married, the one who couldn't seem to get enough of him. But, for now, he thought as he ground against her and heard her groan and beg for more, this would be enough. He'd win her back even if it took snatching away everything that she held dear.

Kim lay on the floor of the solarium, listening to the gentle breathing of her husband against her ear. She wished she could be repulsed by what had happened between them, but her body still tingled from what Troy had done to it. He'd always been an incredible lover. That was never the problem between them. She was turned off by the maleness of him, the memories of being forced to sit on "Uncle" Joe's lap and play horsey when she was only nine years old. That, and Troy's utter lack of drive and entrepreneurial imagination added to her ambivalence. Out of the bedroom, they had nothing in common and over the years, she'd grown to resent him. Not only did she find sexual satisfaction with Stephanie, but the mental stimulation that she so desperately needed. So, now, if she could lull Troy into a sense of well-being, make him believe that there was a chance for them, she could still get hers.

She smiled in triumph when he said he still loved her, no matter what. Yes, she would have it all, she reasoned as she allowed him to enter her again.

CHAPTER FOURTEEN
NO PLACE LIKE HOME

Nicole entered the hot vat of her apartment, the trapped heat nearly knocking her back out the door as it escaped. She sucked in what little air there was, cussed under her breath, and shut the door behind her.

Her sister, Julia, probably heard the word *rain* and shut all the windows on her way out, Nicole thought miserably, wiping a line of perspiration from her top lip.

She trudged into the apartment and walked through the darkened hallway to the bedroom that she still shared with her sister. She plopped down on the bed and stared at the peeling wallpaper that had been there since she was a teenager. Nothing much had changed over the years. The siblings had simply gotten older, moving among each other more out of necessity than desire. Every day was a struggle—trying to keep their heads above water, and the landlord away from their door and out of her panties. Ricky refused to take the money that Nicole offered him from her "jobs." He wouldn't take her dirty money, he'd said, her illegal money. He'd rather live on the street and take his sisters with him.

It would have been so easy for her to move out on her own, live the kind of life that she'd earned on the street. But her conscience wouldn't allow her to leave her family, a debate that sparked many arguments between her and Trust.

"I can take care of you and your *familia*," Trust had said as they lay together in his lush co-op in East Harlem. "You're my woman. I can't have you living like you just got off the boat."

She rolled over, turning her back to him. "I can't leave my family, Trust. They need me."

"Need you! For what? To cook, clean, and take abuse from your brother? He thinks I'm not good enough for you. But if he was any kind of man he would want to make sure that his sisters were well taken care of."

Nicole jumped up from the bed and crossed the room, her young supple body glistening with perspiration from their last lovemaking session. She spun toward him, her full breasts at attention.

"Fuck you! Don't you dare dis my brother! He worked hard all his life to take care of us. He never asked for nothin'. Ricky *is* a man—a good man!" Her dark eyes flashed.

Trust pushed himself into a semi-sitting position. His eyes drifted up and down her body. "All I'm saying is that you can have all this," he murmured, his tone soft and seductive. "Everything you could ever want, I can get it for you. You wouldn't have to share a two-by-four room with your sister or listen to shit from your brother. What could be so wrong with that?"

Nicole swallowed. "Nothing," she snapped and turned away. "I got to go."

"But you'll be back. You always come back. You know this is where you want to be."

She snatched up her discarded clothing and stormed off to the bathroom. She dressed with tears burning her eyes. Trust was right. There was no reason for her and her family to live the way that they did. Pride kept her family a prisoner. She'd stashed away thousands of dollars from her jobs, more money than she'd ever thought she'd have. And the money continued to grow. But what good was it if she could not use it for the very reason she'd gotten involved with Trust in the first place—to make a good life for her family and repay her brother for all his sacrifices?

She'd gotten dressed and walked back out into the master bedroom. Trust was stretched out on the bed. A plume of cigarette smoke floated above his head. He glanced at her through the cloud.

"We got a job tomorrow. I need you to do the driving. I'll call and give you the time and place."

She gave a short nod. "Later," she murmured.

"Yeah, later."

That job had been her last, the one that wound her up in jail doing the time. And there wasn't a day that had gone by since she heard the chilling sound of the metal gates slamming shut behind her that she didn't wonder if Trust had set her up—to teach her a lesson.

Nicole pressed the heels of her palms against her eyes as she inhaled the stale heat. *The mark rarely suspects the ones that are part of their agenda.* She reached in her duffle bag and pulled out her cell phone. She punched in Trust's phone number.

"I want to come back to work," she said in response to Trust's voice. "And . . . I had some time to do some thinking about you and me . . . I'm gonna be coming to stay. Offer still open?"

A cool smile widened Trust's mouth. It was only a matter of time, he mused. "Sure baby. Whatever you want. You know that."

Nicole's heart knocked and pounded in her chest. Ricky would flip, and if her P.O. found out, he could send her back. But it was a chance she had to take, one she was willing to take.

"I'll give you twenty-four hours to get your women in line and out of my spot and then I'll be there—for good." She'd need the time to get things in order.

Trust chuckled. "Not a problem, baby. *Mi casa es su casa.*"

"Make sure that it is." She disconnected the call. There was no turning back now.

CHAPTER FIFTEEN
THE BUSINESS AT HAND

Tracy flipped open the thick manila folder on her desk and slipped on her reading glasses. The documents in front of her outlined the sequence of events that led to the series of raids across the city. Nothing was left to chance—the team carried out their instructions to the letter. And yet, with all the manpower, they had not found the elusive Madam X nor any of her employees.

Tracy shut the folder. There was a piece missing and she was determined to find it. The obvious answer was that there was a leak, and that leak had to come from somewhere in her office or the police department. Her head snapped up at the sound of the knock on her door. She stuck the file in the drawer just as the door opened.

"We need to talk."

The last person she wanted to talk with was her boss, Avery Powell. He was running for reelection as the district attorney, and if she blew this case, she would certainly blow his chances

and, more than likely, her career. She didn't relish the notion of
working in the public defender's office.

"Why don't you come in, Avery," she said, the sarcasm not
going unnoticed.

Avery's jaw clenched. He shut the door. As always, Avery
Powell was dressed impeccably in his role as head crime fighter.
He spared no expense when it came to his attire, and more than
once he'd been featured on the cover of *Gentleman's Quarterly* as
well as a variety of sports magazines that lauded his athleticism.
He was certainly a handsome man: tall—over six feet, with a
solid build, a smooth chestnut brown complexion, and piercing
dark brown eyes framed by thick lashes and slick, sweeping
brows. It was his personality that rubbed Tracy raw. Avery was as
equally arrogant and chauvinistic as he was handsome, and she
still regretted the night she slept with him. Instead of it helping
her career, Avery seemed to take pleasure in making her job as
difficult as possible.

"Madam X . . ."

"Yes?"

He pulled up a seat and sat down without being asked. He
ran the tip of his manicured index finger across his top lip.

"I really need you to explain to me how in the hell this
could have happened." His voice dropped to a threatening low.
"You swore to me that your information was solid." He tossed his
hands up in the air. "And you've delivered zip." The simple end-
ing word was spat out with such venom it sounded like a curse.
He pursed his lips and linked his fingers on top of her desk.

Tracy watched his jaw flex.

"There is too much riding on this. I have every man and
their mother breathing down my neck and wanting answers. I

have nothing to give them. The press would be ecstatic to see slavery reinstituted just so they could see how much they can get for me on the auction block."

"That's a bit extreme, Avery," Tracy said, "I don't think—"

"I don't give a damn what you think!" he said in concert with the pounding of his fist against her desk.

Reflexively, Tracy grabbed her coffee cup as the cooling brown liquid sloshed over the top.

"We'll get her. I promise you that."

Avery stood and looked down at her. "I don't need your promises, Tracy. I need results, or you might as well start getting your resume together. I want an update on my desk." He turned and walked out.

Tracy squeezed her eyes shut and drew in a ragged breath. For several moments she sat motionless, considering her options. This job meant everything to her. She relished the power she had over the lives and liberties of others, the respect she commanded. She was driven to prove herself by any means necessary, a trait that had cost her friendships and her marriage to Scott Alexander. Poor, Scott, she thought. He wanted kids and a quiet life in the suburbs. She wanted her name in lights.

The phone rang.

"Alexander," Tracy answered, bracing the receiver between her shoulder and her ear.

"I just got a call from the mayor's office," Avery said. "He wants this to go away and go away quickly. Do you understand?"

"I'm not going to screw up this investigation and hand over just anybody so it can get thrown out in court," she responded, with the same cool control as Avery. "Not even for the mayor."

"Your do-right agenda will get you about as far as your office door. This is the big time, Tracy. If you can't handle it, I can find someone who can."

She frowned. "Are you taking me off this case?"

"That will be entirely up to you. And I'll be sure to pass your regards onto the mayor over dinner tonight. Or you could attend as my guest and tell him yourself."

"I said I would take care of this, and I will."

"The clock is ticking." Avery hung up the phone.

Tracy uttered a curse under her breath and returned the phone to the cradle. She took off her glasses and massaged the bridge of her nose.

So much was riding on this investigation, she mused, reopening the case folder. She'd staked her reputation on it based on what she believed was solid information. The history of Madam X, as she was called by the authorities, dated back years. She was almost a cult figure in some circles, a folk hero in others. As Tracy came up the ranks in the D.A.'s office and listened to the stories, told almost in awe, she vowed that when the time was right, it would be her that would take Madam X down. The mystique of the madam fascinated as much as repulsed her. Tracy knew that much of the reason for Madam X's elusiveness was that she was protected by the very people who claimed they wanted to rid the city of prostitution: the businessmen, politicians, and the like. She wasn't a fool, and she knew that for the most part she was on this quest alone. Sure, it would look good in the papers and on the late night news, and great on her resume, but the powers that be—other than for political reasons—couldn't care less, a fact that made her job that much more difficult.

Many nights she lay alone in bed, staring at the white-washed ceiling and wondering what made a woman like Madam X do what she did for a living. But, more importantly, why did it matter so much to her? The question dogged her, taunted her in her sleeping and in her waking hours. And one day it hit her. It had nothing to do with ridding the city of crime, or climbing to the top of her profession in the legal world. There was an ugly part of her that simply resented Madam X, resented her with a ferocity that stripped her of any sentiment. She resented the fact that this woman, whoever she was, had a power that Tracy couldn't comprehend. That she had money, homes, men, and an enterprise that rivaled many *Fortune* 500 corporations. And she had it all, not from years of school, sacrifice, and hard work— but from lying on her back and spreading her legs for any man that wanted to take a chance. This woman, this Madam X, was a stain on women everywhere. She perpetuated the myth that women were no more than objects of sex and could be bought for a few dollars and a glass of wine. She was everything that Tracy was not, and perhaps that's what she resented most. But one day she was going to look Madam X in the face and be able to tell her that she, Tracy Alexander, was a better woman than Madam X would ever be. She lived for that moment, prayed for it, and she would have it.

CHAPTER SIXTEEN
6 DEGREES OF SEPARATION

Vincent walked barefoot across the floor of his one-bedroom apartment into the small utilitarian kitchen and turned on the coffeemaker. He leaned against the counter while he waited for the coffee to brew. He folded his arms across his chest and thought about the night before with Tess. He knew this was only a job, another assignment. He'd been trained to disassociate himself from the mark to get the job done. And he was good at it. But Tess had tapped a part of him that he'd kept buried and out of reach.

She was beautiful, funny, intelligent, and one of the sexiest, most alluring women he'd ever met. There was an aura about Tess McDonald that drew you in and enticed you to want to get to know her better. He was pretty sure that she was the woman that they'd been searching for, and he knew that if he played his cards right, this latest assignment would be the pinnacle of his undercover career.

The phone rang, stopping his roaming thoughts.

"Yeah," he said into the phone.

"How much longer is it going to be?" came the reply.

He took a breath and with it a risk. "I, uh . . . I'm not sure."

"What do you mean not sure? Last night you told me you made contact."

"That's what I thought. But I'm not so sure now. I'm gonna need some more time. I need to feel her out. We don't want to make any mistakes and blow this thing," he added.

There was a telling moment of silence on the line.

"Look, don't screw this up. If she's the one, I want you to bring her in. And if you can't we'll get someone in there who can."

"I know what I'm doing! Have I ever fucked up a case?"

"There's a first time for everything. Don't let this be yours. I'm going to give you some time, but I want results. If she's not the one, then you need to find her. Understood?"

"Yeah."

The line disconnected.

Slowly, Vincent hung up and wondered why he'd said what he did. He was as sure that Tess McDonald was Madam X as he was of his own name. He'd had her in his sights for months. Everything added up. But there was one last test. According to his informant, a former client, the Madam had a tattoo of a rose on the upper inside of her left thigh. He planned to find it himself.

CHAPTER SEVENTEEN
DON'T LOOK IN THE MIRROR

Kim stood under the pulsing spray of the shower, hoping to wash away the scent and feel of Troy. She looked down at her cream-toned skin and saw the telltale red indentations of his fingers flaring up along the inside of her thighs, his handprints on her hips, and angry red marks along the crest of her breasts and around the dark pink areolas; reminders that would last for at least a week. A wave of guilty pleasure hardened her clitoris, making it jump and pulse between the slightly swollen lips.

It had been months since she'd had sex with her husband. That was her first mistake. Her relationship with Stephanie had consumed her. She spent all of her free time either with her or thinking about being with her. Stephanie Abrams was her perfect counterpart, matching her stride for stride in brains, energy, ambition, and sexual insatiability.

They'd met three years prior, in San Francisco, at a national journalist and broadcast media conference where Kim was receiving an award. Kim had always heard about the dynamic powerhouse behind the scenes at CNN, but had never had the opportunity to meet her. When Stephanie stepped up to the podium and gave the luncheon keynote address, Kim was mesmerized, and even more so when it was Stephanie who presented Kim with her award of achievement.

Stephanie flashed a smile for the cameras when Kim walked up on stage, but when Kim shook her hand and their eyes connected for a hot, split second they both knew that what was to come was inevitable.

After the luncheon broke up, Stephanie sought Kim out.

"Congratulations," she said, walking up to Kim while she was talking with Collin Perkins, one of the producers of *The Evening Show*.

Kim turned. "Why, thank you."

"Kim, congrats again. I'll catch up with you in New York," Collin said, and disappeared into the crowded ballroom.

"The lunch was crap, as usual," Stephanie said. "Want to find something decent to eat?"

Kim felt a slight thrill, as if she'd been asked on her first date. "Sure. The hotel has a great restaurant."

Over the course of the next few hours, Kim and Stephanie crossed the invisible barrier, the taboo that said the road they were venturing onto was unnatural—a sin. But even the threat of eternal damnation was powerless to stop the thrill of tasting the forbidden fruit.

Stephanie was on her third cosmopolitan, Kim her second apple martini. They were feeling a bit buzzed, a little uninhibited. Conversation flowed freely, as did the extra smiles, and the light touches.

"Are you staying here at the hotel?" Stephanie asked.

"No. I was heading back home. You?"

"I decided to stay in town. I have a room." She gave Kim a long look over the rim of her glass. She took a final sip and set the glass down. "You're welcome to stay with me if you don't feel like making that flight back tonight."

Kim's smile was hesitant. "I . . ." She shrugged. "I suppose I can get a flight out tomorrow. If you're sure you don't mind."

"I wouldn't have asked if I did." She stood. "Come on." She picked up her purse, took out a one-hundred-dollar bill and dropped it on the table. "The drinks are on me." She turned and Kim followed her out.

That night was the first of many. Stephanie was wild and voracious, waking up a part of Kim that had long been dormant. Flying high on good liquor and top-grade cocaine, Stephanie's secret passion, they left no sexual stone unturned. For years, she'd buried her on-again, off-again desire for the feel of another woman. The last thing she needed in her life on her climb up the ladder of success was the albatross of scandal. So she'd stayed in her marriage with Troy, played the dutiful wife and hotshot executive, but there was always something missing. She'd found it with Stephanie.

Kim sighed heavily and stepped out of the shower. The key now was to lull Troy into a sense of security, make him believe that it was over with Stephanie and that their marriage could be saved.

Troy dressed and returned to the chair he'd vacated earlier. Kim truly thought him a fool if she believed an overdue session of sex was going to change anything. True, he still loved her, but he wouldn't let that interfere with what he wanted—*everything that his wife held dear*—and if that included ruining Stephanie Abrams and her politician husband in the process, then so be it.

Every time he thought about the afternoon he'd found out, he wanted to be sick. The private investigator he'd hired had pictures . . . pictures of his wife with Stephanie Abrams. And Troy thought he was going to find out about another man. What a joke.

Troy ran his fingers through his sleek blond hair. Humiliation turned his cheeks a hot pink. The whole world thought him a fool, a kept man. He'd prove them all wrong. He'd show them all who was in charge. And he'd have his wife groveling at his feet. He had no real use for her company, other than to line his pockets and pay his growing gambling debts. But it was the only threat he had that would make her pay attention. She thought of herself as such a wonder woman, let her figure out how to rebuild the house that Kimberly Sheppard built after he'd finished dismantling it. By the time he was done, there wouldn't be anything worth saving, and he'd be long gone.

CHAPTER EIGHTEEN
WHAT HARM COULD IT DO?

Tess stood in front of the full-length mirror that hung on the back of her bathroom door. She always loved how lemon yellow looked against her rich dark skin. The lace bra and matching thong were the perfect undergarment accessories. She turned left, then right, and took a peek over her shoulder. She smiled. "Not bad."

She'd debated for several days over Vincent's invitation for a late dinner under the moon, a drive on the beach—and then whatever happened, happened. Although they'd fallen into a comfort zone of meeting in the evenings to share a walk or a cold bottle of Coors, it never led to more than a brushing of the lips, or hot looks of promise. It was the last part that gave her pause.

She had too much going on to get involved with anyone. When she bedded the men who came through her doors, she knew it was temporary—no emotions, no strings. Vincent was different. For all her bravado, she was seriously turned on by him on several levels, and she knew that going to bed with him might be the corner she wasn't ready to turn just yet. On the other hand, she was physically aching to see just how much of a man he was. She was pretty damned sure that she had enough tricks in her repertoire to blow his natural mind without losing hers.

Tess smiled at her reflection. "Well, as the master crooner, Marvin Gaye, said, "Let's get it on.""

"You look great," Vincent said as Tess slid into his car.

She'd decided on a yellow- and red-splashed wrap skirt that was only held in place by a single knot that rode low on her hip, and a honeysuckle band top that was no more than a cover-up for the lace underneath—both easily undone and accessible, just in case.

"Thanks." She fastened her seat belt and crossed her legs. The fold of the skirt fell open, exposing a polished thigh. She didn't bother to cover up. "Have you decided on dinner?"

Vincent's gaze slid up from her thigh and rested on her knowing smile. "You're more than enough for my appetite, but I figured you'd be hungry, so I actually fixed us a basket of food. I thought we'd eat at the beach."

Her right brow lifted in surprise. "You fixed us dinner?"

"Don't sound so stunned. Or maybe it's alarm I hear." He chuckled and pressed his palm to his chest. "I'm tryin' to convince you that I'm an all-around kinda guy. I even do windows."

Tess tossed her head back and laughed. "You do continue to surprise me."

"I'm like a magician, baby. The outside is all smoke and mir-rors." He winked, put the car in gear, and took off. "You need to get to know the man, not the image."

During the hour-and-a-half ride they talked about everything from politics to their first childhood memory. They debated about the greatest jazz musicians and lauded the accomplish-ments of Muhammad Ali in the ring. They discussed literature and Tess was amazed to discover that Gabriel García Márquez was one of Vincent's favorite authors. They had a long-winded talk about the steady demise of good black literature and the ef-fect of music videos on the youth.

When Tess actually looked up and paid attention to her sur-roundings, Vincent was making the turn into Sag Harbor.

"I have a small houseboat. I rarely get a chance to use it. I thought we could take her out for a while and have dinner on deck."

She angled her head to the side. "I'm almost impressed."

He threw his hands up in mock defeat. "Man, what's a brotha gotta do?" He pulled into a vacant space, got out, and opened her door.

Tess stepped out into the warm sea-washed air and inhaled deeply.

The slowly lapping blue water was dotted with boats of var-ious sizes and levels of splendor, from simple rowboats to full-fledged yachts.

Vincent took the basket out of the trunk.

"Follow me." He proceeded down the boardwalk, passing several impressive boats along the way. "I'm right over there."

He pointed out a beautiful boat with the name "Playa" embla-zoned on the side. He helped her on board. "This is my home away from all the madness."

"Whatever it is that you do, it certainly pays well." She stepped on deck and looked around.

"I do awright. Want the twenty-five-cent tour?"

"Sure."

"Right this way."

He showed her around the upper deck then took her below.

"Full sitting room, stereo, television, and bar." They entered the adjacent room. "This is the galley. I try to keep it pretty well-stocked. Over there is a spare room. Here's the bathroom." He opened a narrow door to a full bathroom. "And back here . . ." he walked farther down and opened the door ". . . is the bedroom." He turned to face her. "Pretty much everything you could want."

"I'd say so. Very nice, Vincent. The ladies must love this."

The corner of his mouth lifted. "Yeah, they seem to," he said, with unabashed confidence. He stepped closer and wrapped one arm around her waist. "What about you?"

"I don't impress easily. But I'll definitely let you know."

Vincent grinned. "You're a tough woman, Tess."

"Not at all. I simply decide what I like, how much, and when. Not complicated at all." She stepped out of his hold. "I think I'll freshen up before we eat."

"Be my guest. I'll be up on deck when you're done." He glanced at her through partially lowered lids before turning and walking out.

Once she was alone, she released a long held breath and took a good look around. It might not be a yacht but it was damned impressive. She'd certainly have to give him points for this little getaway. She never imagined that Vincent was anything more than a handsome face with a body to die for and sex appeal that should be bottled and sold. Now to add to the package, he was intelligent, well read, funny, and obviously had good taste.

Everything about his little hideaway spoke class. There was nothing garish or overstated. The rooms were neat, and decorated in cool colors with contemporary furnishings. Simple and tasteful. This certainly didn't reflect the image that he projected on the street. *Smoke and mirrors.*

Tess placed her hands on her hips and stared along the path that Vincent had taken. There was definitely much more to him than what met the eye. She would have to keep that in mind.

Vincent looked up at Tess's approach. "Just what this baby needed," he said, handing her a glass of white wine. "A beautiful addition."

Tess took the glass. "Thank you." She gazed out onto the water and leaned against the railing. "If this was mine I'd be out here all the time," she said.

"Wish I could. Just not always possible. Ready for a ride?"

"Yes."

Vincent steered the boat along the water with Tess at his side.

"What made you decide to get a boat?" Tess asked.

"Hmmm . . . 'cause none of my friends had one." He laughed. "I've always wanted to be different."

"Are you serious? That's the real reason?"

"It's one of the reasons." He pulled in a breath. "This is gonna sound so lame."

"Then you definitely have to tell me."

"See, when I was a kid, we were real poor—real poor. So our big family vacation was a ride on the Staten Island Ferry. Man, out on that ferry I felt free, with the whole world out in front of me. I promised myself that if I ever got the chance I was gonna have my own boat and have that sense of freedom every chance I could get."

He turned to look at her. "Lame, right?"

"We all have dreams," she said, her tone soft and thoughtful. "Some of us are fortunate enough to make them a reality."

He nodded slowly. "What about you? What dreams do you have?"

Tess pressed her palms against the railing and looked out toward the sea. "I was always too reluctant to dream." She snatched a look at Vincent and quickly looked away. "I figured if I didn't hope for anything I couldn't be disappointed."

Why had she told him that, she wondered the instant the words were out of her mouth. She could have easily said she wanted to be financially independent, or wanted to solve the world's hunger problem, or open a beauty salon. Instead she'd confessed something she'd never said aloud to a soul. It was her silent albatross, the fear of wanting, hoping, and then having it slip away from you. So she lived her life the way she did—no commitments, no promises, no disappointments.

Vincent lowered the anchor and the boat drifted to a stop atop the calm water. The setting sun stretched across the horizon, turning the sea into moving threads of orange and gold. He turned and leaned against the wheel.

"That's the last thing I expected to hear from you," he said. "Why?"

"You seem like the kinda woman who'd have aspirations to land on the moon if given the chance."

"I still am. But I'm not going to be disappointed if I don't get there." She turned to him. "I'm starved."

"Say no more."

They had a mini-feast on deck, complete with wine, light jazz, and the comforting sway of the boat.

"You are talented," Tess said, wiping her mouth with a linen napkin.

"Told you I had skilz." He grinned. "More wine?" He lifted the bottle in question.

"No. I've reached my quota for one evening."

His left brow rose. "So you're ready to be taken advantage of."

Tess laughed. "Oh, the old, 'get her buzzed and take her to bed' routine."

"Wow, you saw right through me." He smirked and finished off his glass of wine.

"Do you really think you need to get me mildly drunk first?"

Vincent leaned across the table. "I'm willing to try anything."

"Why not simply ask?"

A slow smile cinched the corners of his eyes. He stood, came around to her side, took her hand, and guided her to her feet. "I'm gonna make love to you tonight." He pulled her flush against him.

"That doesn't sound like a question."

"Wasn't meant to be. Not really my style."

He lowered his head until he was a breath away from her mouth. "Come downstairs and I'll show you what I want to do to you."

Tess tried to recall the last time she was seduced, when she was made to feel she was the most important thing in the world and that her pleasure was the priority. Too long, she realized, as Vincent made slow, deliberate work of removing her scant outfit, burning her exposed skin with brushes of his lips, and murmuring how beautiful she was.

When he stepped out of his clothes, she kept her delight in check. This was going to be a night he would never forget, Tess silently vowed. What she had in mind for him would take hours and have him calling for the Father in heaven when she was done.

If she wasn't a professional, she needed to have her stuff patented, Vincent thought as she rotated her hips to meet his every move. For a hot minute he saw stars and totally forgot that it was only a job. Every square inch of him felt like it was on fire. He couldn't begin to describe what she'd done to him. He felt delirious with pleasure that wouldn't stop, but kept reaching crescendos, only to bring him back down and then up again for another assault on his senses and his willpower. He wanted to scream, beg her to let him come, but the pleasure was so intense all he could do was moan her name and who knows what else.

And when she finally showed mercy and his orgasm hit, his entire body experienced a kind of paralysis as the very essence of him jettisoned out of his body. A strangled groan burst from his chest as she squeezed and contracted around him, and he shook as if electrocuted until the tremors subsided and he fell limply against her.

Tess held him, her legs wrapped tightly around his waist. She stroked his hair and smiled triumphantly as she listened to the racing of his heart.

What seemed like hours later, Vincent found the strength to ease out of her and roll onto his back. He stared up at the ceiling in disbelief. If he had good sense he'd get up, run and never look back.

Thinking about what she'd done to him had him ready again. He turned on his side. "Your turn," he said in a harsh whisper.

Tess enveloped him with her smile.

"I'm gonna see if I can drag myself out of this bed and get a shower before we head back," Vincent said. He pushed himself up into a sitting position.

Tess stretched, long and slow. "I'll be here when you get back."

Vincent leaned over and ran his hand along the dip in her waist and then the rise of her hip. He caressed the weight of her breasts and ran his tongue along the tempting nipples.

"That's what I'm afraid of," he said. He stood, gave her a wink, and walked down the narrow hall to the bathroom.

Tess put her hands behind her head and laughed. "Whatever this turns out to be, it was damned sure fun getting here."

The faint sound of running water could be heard in the distance. Tess snuggled up against the pillow. She liked him, she truly did, with all of his arrogance and urban cool. He was totally refreshing and exciting—something she could use in her life.

Who was she fooling? She was in no position to entertain the thought of a relationship. But, at least for the time being, she could pretend that she was just like every other woman, and enjoy it while she could.

The sudden shrill ring of the telephone interrupted her musings. Probably one of his women, she thought, glancing toward the nightstand.

On the fourth ring, she heard Vincent's voice in the distance and realized that the answering machine was in the adjoining room.

But it wasn't a woman who responded to his invitation to leave a message.

"I need some answers," the authoritative male voice said.

Tess slowly sat up in the bed, straining to hear.

"I want to hear from you first thing in the morning. I mean it."

The call disconnected.

Old habits die hard, Tess mused as she got up from the bed, listened to make sure the water was still running and went into the next room. She replayed the tape. It was clear by the caller's tone that Vincent had pissed him off. Who was Vincent, really?

She glanced toward the bathroom door.

She returned to the bedroom. Her eyes darted around the semidarkened space. In her early days she'd rolled a few of her clients, and she hadn't lost a beat as she systematically went through the closet and drawers for any clues.

Nothing of any interest, other than a .38 tucked away in a shoebox. But even she had one of those.

She put everything back the way she found it, just as she heard the shower water stop. She returned to sit on the side of the bed, moments before Vincent returned.

"All yours," he said, running a towel across his damp hair.

"Thanks."

"There's clean towels on the shelf in the bathroom."

She stood and walked toward the door.

Vincent clasped her upper arm. "I want to keep seeing you, Tess."

She gave him a half smile. "You might want to check your messages. You had a call while you were in the shower." She ran a smooth nail down the center of his chest and walked out.

Vincent stood for a moment in the center of the room. Tess Mc-Donald was, without question, the woman he was looking for. He'd seen the tattoo. All it would take now was a simple phone call and this would be over and he could move on to the next assignment.

He glanced at the phone, saw the flashing red light and pressed "play." As he listened, he thought about Tess, the woman he was getting to know, and thought about the feelings he could no longer fight. He picked up the phone and started to dial.

The sound of Tess singing in the shower stopped him midway. Slowly, he replaced the receiver. Just a little while longer, he thought, dancing on that dangerous tightrope of duty and emotion. Maybe a day or two more—just to be with her. Then he'd do what he'd been hired for. He knew it was going to be the toughest decision of his career.

CHAPTER NINETEEN
THE TIES THAT BIND

"*Hijo*, we need to talk," Nicole said to Ricky as she walked into the kitchen the following morning.

Ricky looked up from reading the paper and put down his cup of coffee. "*Que eso?*"

Nicole pulled a chair out from beneath the table and sat down. "I've been doing some thinking . . . about my life and stuff."

"Yeah."

"I know that I was released into your custody until I found my own place."

His smooth caramel features hardened by degrees. His jaw flexed. "What is this about, Nikki?"

"I'm . . . I got me a place to stay."

"Oh really. Where?" His dark eyes bored into hers, daring her to lie.

She focused on the tabletop and the circular ring his cup was making on the surface. "A little further uptown."

"You're lyin'. I can always tell when you're lyin' cause you

can't look me in the eye. Look me in the eye, Nikki, and tell me
your bullshit story again."

Her head snapped up. Her mouth worked but no words
came out.

"Yeah, just like I thought." He pushed back from the table
and stood, knocking the cup over in the process. He ignored
the mess. "You barely been home a month and you already
itchin' to get back with that bum! The same one who got you
locked up. You wanna go back to that hellhole, is that the
deal? What's wrong wit you?" He threw his hands up in the air,
then ran them through his chin-length hair. "Where was he
when you was locked up all them months?" He paced in front
of her. "Who came to see you? Me and your sister! I didn't
have to take you in. But I did, because you're my family and I
swore at our parent's gravesite that I would take care of my sisters until my last breath. And this is what you want to do?" His
face had turned a deep red as a vein pulsed dangerously in his
neck.

Nicole's head began to swirl with the images of prison, the
feeling of fear and humiliation that gripped her daily, even as
Ricky's voice pounded against her trying to get past the wall of
visions that still held her prisoner.

As if propelled, she jumped up from the chair, slamming her
palms against the tabletop. "You know nothing!" she screamed
and kicked the chair to the floor. "I was the one in there day after day. I was the one who was beaten and raped." She saw the
shock in his eyes. "Yes, raped, with things you can't begin to
imagine, and beaten if I didn't take it like a woman." Her voice
cracked as her chest rose and fell in uneven beats. "Me, *hijo*, and
you know why? 'Cause I wouldn't tell them what they wanted to

know about Trust. So I did the time and he let me." Her body shuddered. She looked at her brother with eyes that blazed with something unimaginable. "He let me. And for that, he must pay." The words were said with such sudden calm that Ricky felt chilled. "I can't do that here. *Comprende?* To catch a thief you live among them." She turned and her ponytail whipped around her shoulders. "You can decide to disown me, call my P.O. and turn me in. That's your choice." She turned to face him. "And this is mine."

He looked at his sister, perhaps really seeing her for the first time in years. "*Por favor*, you don't have to do this Nikki. You don't have to go back there. Go to the *policia*."

She shook her head. "No. The *policia* can't do what I can do. I go to them, tell them all that I know, they arrest Trust, he finds a way out and comes after me or my *familia*. No. I have a better way."

"What way?"

"An eye for an eye, *hijo*. An eye for an eye."

He lowered his head to his raised palms, then looked up at his sister. "Vengeance is mine, sayeth the Lord."

"He'll forgive me."

"But will you ever forgive yourself?"

The question caught her off guard. She hadn't thought about how or what she would feel. Her every thought and action was fueled by rage and bitterness. That's all she knew—all she would accept.

"It doesn't matter." She stood. "I'm going to make it right, Ricky." She turned and walked out of the room.

Moments later, she heard the front door slam shut.

Nicole entered her bedroom. She had to hurry. She didn't

want to have to look into the eyes of her sister and explain where she was going. Telling Ricky had been painful enough.

She went to the closet, pulled out the battered suitcase and began packing her belongings. As she sifted through what she would take and what she would leave, an odd level of excitement flooded her veins.

No longer would she have to worry about the expensive clothes she put on her body and her brother's accusing eye, or ride the train anymore and pray that a derelict didn't rub up against her. She could walk through the neighborhood and get back her respect. She'd be back in the life, in the heat of the action. She could resurrect her old contacts while keeping her eye on her goal.

After putting as much as she could in the suitcase, she took a wobbly white wooden chair from the corner and brought it back to the closet. Standing on the less-than-stable seat, she felt along the side wall of the closet above the top shelf until the poster-board panel came away.

Nicole stretched until she located her knapsack, the one that contained her gun and her money. She took the bag out and put the panel back in place just as she heard the front door open.

Quickly, she jumped down from the chair, shut the closet door, and put the chair back in the corner.

"Hey, Nik." Her sister Julia walked into the room. She tossed her backpack on the bed, and followed behind it, landing spread-eagle.

Nicole chuckled. She was still so sweet.

"Whew, long day." She flipped onto her back. "What are you doing home, anyway? "Didn't you get your job back at the dentist?"

"Naw." She shrugged. "Doc told me it took too long for me to get back from buying that pack of cigarettes." Her dry laugh held no joy. "He hired someone else."

Julia sat up. "Sorry. But you'll find something."

"Yeah."

"What's up with the suitcase?"

Nicole's gaze crossed the room. "I need to talk to you." She came and sat down next to Julia. "Listen, I'm going to be leaving."

Julia's voice rose an octave when she asked why. "You don't have to go back, do you?" Her question was more of a plea, and for an instant Nicole second-guessed her decision.

"You can't leave us again," Julia cried. "It would kill Ricky. Don't you care about anybody but you?" Anxiety darkened her sand-toned skin.

"Julia, I'm not going back. But this is something I have to do. I swear to you on mama's and papa's graves." She made a quick sign of the cross and stared into her sister's eyes. She cupped Julia's soft cheeks in her hands. Tears dripped over Nicole's fingers.

"You just got home. You haven't been back a good month yet. You don't know how much we missed you," she said, her voice halting and tremulous. She looked at Nicole. "I was so scared. And . . . embarrassed. The kids in school would tease me about having a sister in jail. They'd tell me horrible things that would happen to you in there and that you would come out more a man than a woman." She sniffed hard. "I had to defend you. I had to tell them they were lying about you. Tell me they were lying. Tell me!"

Nicole swallowed hard. "Yes, they were lying." She pulled her sister close. "They were lying." Gently, she stroked her back

the way she used to when Julia was little and couldn't sleep and
the only one who could settle her down was Nicole.

From the moment of her arrest, and the numerous court ap-
pearances, and throughout the trial, sentencing, and incarcera-
tion, she never truly digested what a toll it all took on her
family. She'd taken her entire family on the nightmare ride with
her. They were innocent, but had done the time as surely as if
they'd each done what she'd been convicted of. She had to
make that right.

"I'm sorry," Nicole whispered. "Please forgive me."

Julia nodded her head against Nicole's chest. Slowly, she
eased out of her sister's embrace. "If you're not going back,
where are you going?"

Nicole's heart tightened in her chest. "Things I need to do,
that's all. But I'll come by and see you. I swear."

Julia jumped up from the bed and stomped across the room,
then spun toward her sister. The tears rolled freely down her
cheeks as she stood in front of her sister.

"You're going back to him, aren't you?"

"You know how you said you had to defend me, make them
take back what they said about me?"

"Sí."

"That's what I need to do now, Julia. I need to defend myself. And you know how you can help me? Find a decent guy
who will love and cherish you and not use you," she said, the
last words taut and biting.

Understanding seemed to age her sixteen-year-old sister.
The innocent light in her eyes dimmed and the soft curves of
her face took on a chisled look.

Nicole's insides twisted in confusion and doubt. She didn't

want to hurt her sister. That wasn't her intent. She wanted to make sure that Julia never had to experience what she went through, and making sure that men like Trust were out of the way was a means to an end. It might hurt Julia for a little while, but she'd get over it. She would make it all up to her when this was over and behind her.

She reached out and took Julia's hand.

"It's gonna be all right," she whispered. "I promise you. I don't want you to worry."

Julia tugged her hand away and looked into her sister's eyes. "I don't believe you." She turned and stormed off into the bathroom, locking the door behind her.

For several moments Nicole stood in the center of the room. Indecision held her in place. She had a choice to make. Stay, and satisfy her sister and brother, or leave and satisfy herself so that she could finally have peace. She knew once she walked out that door and back into the life, it was the point of no return.

She walked over to the bed, looked over her belongings, zipped up the suitcase, and walked out.

CHAPTER TWENTY

PIECES OF THE PUZZLE

Kimberly had a full day ahead of her. There was a major staff meeting that afternoon and she wanted to be prepared. She'd worked at home for part of the morning and was finally en route to her office. Stopping for a light, she saw her building up ahead. She made a split-second decision, flashed her left turn signal, and sped off toward the Eastside of Manhattan. Even if Stephanie wouldn't answer her calls, she wouldn't dare turn her away in person. They needed to talk.

The receptionist at CNN glanced up from her horseshoe-shaped desk. She adjusted her headset.

"Yes, may I help you?" She smiled benignly.

"I need to see Stephanie Abrams."

"Do you have an appointment?"

It was quite apparent that although this young slip of a woman worked for a major cable network, she obviously didn't watch much television or read, Kim thought in annoyance.

"Please tell her that Kimberly Sheppard-Benning is here to see her and that I'm willing to wait."

The young woman's eyes suddenly widened in recognition. She pressed her hand to her chest.

"I'm so sorry," she profusely apologized. "I didn't realize . . ." she stuttered as she adjusted her headset yet again and began punching numbers into the phone console.

"Hi, Marie. Ms. Sheppard-Benning is here to see Stephanie." Her gaze rose up to look at Kim, then back to the console. "She said she'd wait." She glanced at Kim again, her look apologetic. "Okay, thanks, Marie."

She disconnected the call and put on a toothpaste-commercial smile. "Mrs. Abrams is in a meeting, but it's scheduled to wrap up in about ten minutes. You're welcome to wait for Mrs. Abrams in the lounge."

"Thank you."

The young woman rose. "I'll—"

"I know my way." She gave her a tight smile.

Kimberly proceeded down the short hallway and turned into the lounge. Thankfully, it was empty, and she wouldn't have to look like all the other nervous ninnies who sat with bated breath, waiting to be called.

She fixed herself a cup of coffee while she waited and wondered: What would Stephanie's reaction be when they faced each other for the first time since the phone call, several weeks earlier?

"Excuse me, Mrs. Benning."

Kimberly turned toward the door to see the secretary standing in the threshold.

"Mrs. Abrams will see you now."

Oh, she will, will she, Kimberly thought, inwardly fuming at being made to feel no more than an inconvenience. She took up her purse from the couch and followed the young woman out.

The closer she got to Stephanie's office, the more determined she became to make sure that Stephanie did what was needed of her.

The secretary tapped lightly on the door, opened it, and stepped inside. Kimberly walked in.

Stephanie barely glanced up from her computer screen.

Kimberly closed and locked the door behind her.

Stephanie's fingers stilled over the computer keys. "You shouldn't have come here."

"You didn't leave me much choice."

Kimberly crossed the room and stopped on the opposite side of Stephanie's mammoth desk.

"I want to make sure you listen."

"Listen to what? There's nothing to say. I told you where I stood with this. I'm not going to ruin Malcolm. And neither will you. I want this to all go away. And if it takes you getting out of my life, then so be it." She turned cold green eyes on Kimberly and slowly stood. "For good."

Kimberly's stomach rose to her throat. A sharp pain followed. As she stood there looking at this woman for whom she'd loved and sacrificed, she realized she had no idea who Stephanie Abrams really was.

A cruel smile formed along the corners of Kimberly's mouth.

"I see. Just like that." She snapped her fingers and began to move around to Stephanie's side of the desk. "I don't think so, Stephanie."

Stephanie took a step back. "Get out."

"No."

"I'll call security."

"Do that." She laughed. "I'll cause a scene that will rival 'live at eleven.' You see, Steph, I suddenly realized I don't have a damned thing to lose. You do. Malcolm does." She shrugged. "So now that you want me out of your life, why should I give a lousy shit about what happens to you and your husband?"

Stephanie's cheeks flamed red, as if she'd been slapped.

"You don't want a scandal any more than I do," Stephanie said, minus her earlier bravado.

Kimberly reached around Stephanie and turned the wand on the floor-to-ceiling blinds until they closed.

"As I said, nothing can hurt me now. I can handle it, and Troy will get over his embarrassment." She reached out and un-buttoned the top of Stephanie's blouse.

Stephanie's voice was tight and strained. "What are you doing?"

"Saying good-bye. And while I do," she finished with the buttons, "you're going to do as I tell you." She pushed the blouse over Stephanie's shoulders and down her arms. Her eyes drifted to the rise and fall of Stephanie's breasts in her lacy bra.

"Hmm, green, my favorite color."

Stephanie moaned deep in her throat as Kimberly eased her up on the desk.

She knew every square inch of Stephanie and knew her weaknesses. She smiled. "I thought you didn't want me anymore."

"I lied," Stephanie murmured.

Forty minutes later, Kimberley emerged from Stephanie's

office. Her face was flushed and her eyes a bit bright, the only signs of what transpired.

She tugged on the hem of her jacket and checked her purse to be sure her package was tucked securely inside.

Stephanie couldn't stop shaking. She could still feel the heat of Kim's body against hers. Turning to face the window, she opened the blinds and peered down from the thirty floors above, wondering if Kim was among the throng.

She turned away, hugging her arms around her body. She'd never known Kim to be so cold and deliberate. Perhaps she'd been blinded by the soft feminine side that Kim presented to her. Today, Kim showed the ruthless, calculating side of her that had taken her up the ladder of success.

Slowly, Stephanie crossed the room and sat down on the couch. Kim was right, Malcolm and the media must never find out.

CHAPTER TWENTY-ONE

REVELATIONS

From the moment Tracy set foot in her office that morning it had been a nonstop, grueling series of events. She'd presented her closing argument three days earlier on a major drug case and the jury came back that morning with a guilty verdict on all counts. The court erupted into chaos and security was brought in to bring everyone under control. The two defendants were part of a much bigger organization, but as three-time offenders, and with the Rockefeller Law in place, they wouldn't breathe free air ever again.

The press conference following the verdict was exhausting, but she'd stood her ground. The reporters were relentless.

"Ms. Alexander, I understand that threats have been made against your life as a result of you trying this case," one reporter said.

Tracy straightened her shoulders. "Threats, unfortunately, are part of the job. But that's all they are—threats. If I was to back down every time I received a death threat, I'd never accomplish anything. I won't be intimidated. That's not what the people pay me for."

"And what about the Madam X case?" shouted another reporter.

"Our sources indicate that we are very close," Tracy said. "I'm keeping a close watch on this one." She looked directly into the camera. "When I took on this job, I made a promise to the people of New York and myself that I would find the criminals, prosecute them, and put them away. I'm a woman of my word."

"Do you plan on arresting and pressing charges against the johns, as well, when you get Madam X?"

"I will do whatever is necessary. Thank you." She turned and walked back into her office building.

That was the least of her concerns, she thought, as the press conference replayed in her head. For every victory there was always a defeat.

She stared unblinking at the documents in front of her. She'd gone over every page, every bit of collected evidence, every photograph hoping that it was all some macabre mistake. But a part of her always knew that Tess was the woman she'd been looking for—her sister, her flesh and blood. She'd put the pieces together herself over time; Tess's extravagant lifestyle, the travel, clothes, men, and money—on a stewardess's salary—not hardly. The truth made her ill.

A sudden rush of bile rose to her throat and sent her running to her private bathroom. She lost track of how long she stayed on her hands and knees purging her anguish, anger, and total sense of betrayal.

Finally, she pulled herself up off the floor, splashed cold water on her face, and rinsed her mouth. She glanced up and into the murky mirror and pulled in long cleansing breaths.

My God, what was she going to do? As an officer of the court, she was bound by oath and duty to protect the citizens that she represented from people like Tess McDonald—her sister.

Her throat ached. She covered her face with her hands and wept.

The sudden ringing of the phone jerked her out of her despair. She wiped her eyes with a tissue. Slowly, she left the bathroom and answered the phone.

"Alexander," she said by rote.

Silence.

Tracy frowned in annoyance. "Hello?"

Nothing.

She hung up.

The sound of metal wheels clanging along the marble floors of the hallway broke into the silence. She glanced at the circular clock—standard city issue—that hung above her office door. Ten-thirty. Other than herself, and now the cleaning crew, there was certainly no one on staff around.

She rubbed her eyes and slowly rotated her stiff neck.

"Still here, Ms. Alexander?"

Tracy looked at the opened door and smiled. "Yes, Pete. Long day."

"Will you be much longer? I want to get in there and vacuum the rug."

"Your timing is perfect. I'll be ready in about fifteen minutes."

He nodded. "I'll come back then."

She got up and closed her office door, then went back to her desk, sat down, and picked up the phone before she had time to think about the ramifications.

She closed her eyes and listened to the phone ring on the other end.

"Hello?"

"Tess, it's Tracy."

Tess pressed the button on the remote and lowered the volume of the television.

"Hmmm, and to what do I owe the pleasure?"

"I know who you really are, Tess." Her tone was cool and detached.

Tess sputtered a laugh. She sat straight up in the chair. "Of course you know who I am. Have you been drinking?" She stood and began to pace. She reached for a cigarette and lit up.

"They're going to put you away, Tess."

She blew a cloud of smoke into the air, and then another.

"What exactly are you talking about?"

"You're Madam X. And don't waste your time or mine denying it." Her laugh was derisive. "Under my nose all these years. What a fool you must have thought I was. How many nights did you spend laughing at me?"

"Tracy . . . this is not about you."

"Isn't it? Isn't this simply another way to thumb your nose at me, make light of what I do, what I believe in? It's always been this way between us."

"You still don't get it," Tess said with resignation. "It was never about you having to measure up. It was about me! Me, Tracy."

"What are you talking about?" she countered.

"Next to you I was always a second-class citizen. You were

always perfect in everything. Always *good*. You think I didn't know that you were daddy's favorite?" Her voice rose in pitch and cracked with emotion. "You think I didn't hear him whisper to you at night when he tucked us in and barely patted my head? Or how the teachers could tell us apart—oh yes, Tess, the troublesome one, or Tracy, the smart one. How anything I asked for from mama was always rationed out like food stamps, not with any love or care. All you had to do was walk in a room and could have anything you wanted."

"Tess . . ."

"So I made my own way, Trace. Did my own thing. Pulled so far away from you and your ideals and your perfection that we'd never have to compete at anything ever again."

"Compete? Your life, my life—all comes down to competition?"

"Guess what—in this game everyone loses." She crushed out her cigarette in the overflowing ashtray and lit another one.

"You made a choice, Tess. This is the life you chose, an illegal one. You can't get away with it."

"I could . . . if you let me. You could make the evidence disappear. And I'd get out of your life for good. No one would ever know," she said, her voice dipping to a hypnotic whisper.

"You know I can't do that. I won't do that."

"Not even for your own flesh and blood?"

Tracy swallowed. "No."

"Humph. I didn't think so." She put out her cigarette. Her eyes filled. "Take care, Trace."

Tracy listened to the dial tone hum in her ear. Blindly, she hung up the phone, as tears rolled down her cheeks. "Damn you, Tess."

For as long as Tracy could remember, she and Tess had been at odds with each other. Their mother, God rest her soul, often told them that even in the playpen they fought. It was true what Tess said about their parents, and over time Tracy learned how to milk and manipulate them both, taking a quiet pleasure in Tess's isolation. She never considered what it was doing to her sister. All that concerned Tracy was being better. Had she in some way contributed to the life that Tess chose? Was it possible that Tess sought the attention and accolades of others because she never got it at home? No. She would not take the blame. Life was about choices. They'd each made their own choices for their own reasons.

She stood and walked to the window, looking out at the twinkling lights of Manhattan. How different would both their lives have been if they had truly been sisters in every sense of the word?

Regret, sadness, and the unfamiliar sensation of defeat took up residence in her soul. All these years she'd harbored such resentment and jealousy over her "fabulous" sister only to discover that Tess was truly no different than she. Both of them were seeking validation from everything and everyone other than themselves.

She turned toward her desk. The documents called out to her.

She snatched up the folder and walked over to the shredder. For a brief moment she contemplated what she was about to do. Her career would end. All that she worked for, sacrificed for, would end.

Before she could change her mind she pressed the button, and the folder and all its contents were reduced to scraps.

Tracy returned to her desk, pulled out a sheet of stationery, and wrote her letter of resignation to Avery.

She could always leave New York and open a practice in some small town, she thought, as her heels clicked against the marble floors. She stopped in front of Avery's office, paused a moment, then slid the envelope under the door. She continued down the hall to the elevator.

Tracy stepped out into the night. She looked around at the deserted street, then behind her to the building that had become her home. Slowly, she walked down the stairs for the last time.

She'd start over, she thought, as she walked the two long blocks to the parking lot. She'd start over, and with no evidence against her sister, maybe Tess would start over as well.

"Excuse me."

Tracy slowed to a stop.

"Can you tell me which way is the A train?"

"Sure, it's a block back that . . ." In that instant she knew something was terribly wrong. The scream was trapped in her dry throat. The last thing she saw was the flash of the gun, a millisecond before the bullet slammed into her chest.

Her final thought, before darkness engulfed her, was that she'd finally done the right thing at the end.

Tess paced the small confines of her apartment. She'd finished off a half-pack of cigarettes and knew she'd never make it through the night without a quick run to the corner store. One of the perks of living in the hood—there was a twenty-four-hour store on every other corner.

As she walked along the darkened streets, passing several local businesses, she wondered why, in this totally black community, the businesses were all run by every other ethnic group but African-Americans.

She'd been so removed over the years from day-to-day urban life, traveling in the stratosphere of the upper echelon of society, it never occurred to her to take a closer look at what was happening to the people who were at the root of who she was. To her, crime, homelessness, poverty, and drugs were merely news articles and highlights of television broadcasts.

But now that she was at the epicenter of black life in its rawest form, she was forced to see a life that she'd pushed to the back of her mind, like an old pair of useless shoes to a corner of the closet.

Yet, skirting above the surface of the overflowing trash, loud music, teenage girls pushing baby carriages, and deals made on schoolyard street corners, was a vibrancy and regalness that could not be denied. The stately brownstones still held their charm along with their history; the seniors still dressed in their best simply to go out to get the daily newspaper; and the old gents still sat around a card table, or gathered in the local barbershop and tipped their hats when a woman went by. There was an unspoken unity here. Even those not bound by blood were bound by a common denominator—being black in America. It was them against the world.

This was the world that her sister dealt with and fought for every day, her one-woman campaign to regain the sense of brother and sisterhood that had once made us such a mighty race. A wave of unexpected empathy flowed through her.

For years she'd simply dismissed Tracy's zeal as being naïve and self-righteous. Perhaps she *was* part of the problem that Tracy fought to correct.

She stopped in the store, made her purchase, and slowly returned to her apartment, her thoughts of the future and the events she had set into motion dogging her steps and her conscience.

Why had Tracy bothered to call? It wasn't because she cared. She called to gloat. To throw it in her face that she'd beaten her once again—that she was better. She'd rather see her ruined, imprisoned, than to part with her ideals.

Her sister. Her chest tightened. Understanding suddenly broke through the decades-old layers of jealous irrationality. Tracy'd called to warn her!

She had to stop them. But which one? Which one had Tracy?

Tess ran back into the living room to get her cell phone. She had to warn her sister. *Oh, God.* Her fingers trembled as she punched in the numbers.

While the phone rang, her gaze drifted to the television. The newscaster was mouthing words she could not hear. But Tracy's head-shot was on the screen.

Tess reached for the remote and turned up the volume.

"Police are at the crime scene where the body of Assistant District Attorney Tracy Alexander was found only moments ago . . ."

The remote crashed to the floor, the batteries spilling out

and vanishing beneath the sofa. Everything moved in slow motion—the good, the bad, the blood they shared.

An incredible ache entered her soul, opening up a chasm so deep her wail echoed through every crevice, every vein, to pour out onto the street below. The game had begun and she couldn't stop it. What had she done?

CHAPTER TWENTY-TWO

MAKE IT GO AWAY

Every newspaper and television broadcast was filled with the brutal murder of Assistant District Attorney Tracy Alexander. District Attorney Avery Powell made a plea to the public to come forward with any information that would lead to the arrest and conviction of the murderer.

"Ms. Alexander was a true champion of the people," he intoned. "We will find out who did this and they will pay."

Tess turned off the television and stared sightlessly at the blank screen. Tracy was dead. She covered her face with her hands.

Her cell phone rang. Absently, she answered.

"Hello."

"Hey doll. It's Vincent."

"Now is not a good time, Vincent."

"Are you okay?"

Her throat tightened. "No."

"I'm right on the corner. Can I come up?"

"Vincent . . ."

"I'm coming up. Answer the door."

He disconnected the call.

Tess pulled herself up off the couch, made her way into the bathroom, and splashed some water on her face. She glanced up into the mirror. Inhaling deeply, she drew on her inner resolve. She'd set this deadly game into motion and now was compelled to follow through. If she didn't, all of the players would surely come tumbling down.

The doorbell rang.

Tess dried her face, ran her fingers through her short hair, and went to the door.

The instant Vincent looked into Tess's eyes he knew something was wrong.

"You've been crying."

"Mood swing," she said off-handedly, and stepped aside to let him in.

"Really?" He didn't sound convinced.

"One of those days. What can I tell you? Thirsty?" She kept her back to him.

"No. I'm fine." He walked up behind her and put his arms around her waist. "I can't stop thinking about you," he said against the back of her neck.

She drew in a breath and closed her eyes as his warm breath seemed to breathe life back into her body. She relaxed against him.

"Is that a good thing?"

He turned her around. "A very good thing." He brushed her cheek with the pad of his thumb. "What can I do to make it better, Tess, whatever it is that's bothering you?"

She leaned up and kissed him gently on the mouth. No man

had ever asked her that, cared enough or mattered enough. For a moment she was at a loss. She took his hand and led him to her bedroom and did the only thing she really knew how to do, blow a man's mind and give herself a moment of peace in the process.

CHAPTER TWENTY-THREE

THIS IS FOR REAL

Nicole moved around the lush apartment, reacquainting herself with the surroundings. She and Trust had spent many a night and long morning in this place. But she knew this was only a diversion. He conducted all his business at his place farther uptown. He thought she didn't know anything about his little hideaway, but there wasn't much that Nicole didn't know about Trust.

She went into the kitchen and searched the fridge for something to eat. For most of the day she'd stayed indoors, glued to the television.

When she'd come in late last night, Trust wasn't there. And for a hot minute, she thought that maybe. . . . But, the news that morning was filled with the murder of Tracy Alexander.

There was a citywide hunt for the killer or killers, the news announcer said.

Nicole brought the glass of juice to her lips and noticed her hands were shaking. Nothing to worry about, she told herself.

Tomorrow, she would be back to work at the shop. Trust said that a few new arrivals were waiting for her magic touch.

She smiled. Yeah, it was all good.

The orange glow of the setting sun moved across the expanse of the hardwood floors. Rapper Fat Joe played a driving beat in the background. The air was filled with the pungent smell of weed.

Trust took a long hit from the pipe and passed it to Monroe.

"This is some good stuff," Monroe murmured.

"You know I only get the best." He leaned back against the oxblood leather headrest of the sectional couch.

Monroe chuckled. "That's why you have East Harlem on lockdown. You the man."

"I learned from the best. Fetch was no joke."

"God rest his soul."

"One thing he always taught me though, and I'll never forget." He took another hit before speaking. "The only person you can ever really trust is yourself."

Monroe's vision cleared long enough to take a good look at his friend. He laughed nervously. "Whatchu sayin', man?"

"I'm saying what I just said. Did I stutter?"

"Naw, man, I'm just—"

"I want you to keep an eye on Nikki."

A moment of relief eased the knot in the center of his chest. He almost smiled. "Sure, boss, no problem. Anything I need to know?"

Trust pursed his lips and absently played with the diamond stud in his ear. "Got a feelin' she's playin' me, man."

"With another dude?" His features creased in disbelief. He chuckled. "Not Nikki, man."

"Somethin's up." He opened his eyes. They were cold and flat, like stones. "She ain't actin' right behind closed doors. *Comprende?*"

Monroe's eyes widened with understanding. Slowly, he nodded his head. "So what you want me to do if I find something—somebody?"

Trust cut his gaze in Monroe's direction. "Bring him to me."

"And what about Nikki?"

"I'll deal with her."

Monroe was thoughtful for a moment, knowing how volatile Trust could be when provoked, and even more so when he was loaded. He took a chance.

"I know this ain't really none of my business, bro, but we been boys for a long time so I'm'a say my piece then leave it alone."

"Yeah, awright. I'm listenin'." He leaned toward the glass table, cut a line of coke with a razor, and made every grain vanish through his trademark gold straw.

"All I'm sayin' is Nikki has always been cool, been in your corner from the gate. Come on, man, she took the fall for you, bro. She coulda rolled ovah on you, but she didn't."

"That don't mean jack! I know what I know," he boomed, pounding on his chest for emphasis. "I want you on her ass twenty-four-seven. I want you to hand me the motha that's beatin' my time." His smooth features twisted into an ugly mask of rage.

Monroe held up his hands. "Awright, awright. I gotchu."

"Yeah, that's better." He leaned forward, reached for the glassine bag, poured more of the white powder onto the table and finished it off. He sat back and sniffed long and hard, closing his eyes as the powerful rush exploded in his body. The right corner of his mouth lifted into a semblance of a grin. "Good stuff," he mumbled.

The two men silently rocked to the beat of the music as the drugs flowed through their veins.

Trust sat up, totally energized. "Yo, man, Nikki's up at the crib, waitin' on me. But I got some business over here to take care of. Why don't you do me a solid and take her out for a few hours. Keep her busy, see what's what, ya know."

"Ah, yeah, sure." Monroe reluctantly stood up, stretched and reached for his jacket. "What time you want me to have her back at the crib?"

His glance slid toward his friend. "It may be a long night . . . take your time." He grinned.

Monroe looked at Trust for a moment, nodded, and walked out. He had better things to do than babysit.

Trust stretched. He had plans for the night and didn't want to have to concern himself with Nicole. Monroe was right. He had nothing to worry about when it came to Nicole. She was true to the game and to him. He had his doubts initially. But since she'd been back, it was just like old times. The fact still remained that he always had a penchant for variety. Simply because his woman was back home didn't change his reality.

So, tonight he planned to entertain a new bundle of goods

that he'd met in the club about a week earlier. He didn't usually go for her type, but he'd try anything once.

He took out a bottle of wine and put it in the ice bucket to chill, selected some CDs and put them in the machine. He took a quick look around. He smiled. She would be very impressed. They all were.

He decided to take another hit before his guest arrived and was just finishing up when the doorbell rang.

"It's showtime."

"Why don't you try a little of this?" she said once they were settled and relaxing on the couch. "It will get you in the mood."

"I'm always in the mood, baby. But I'll give you a play." He took a dip from the coke spoon she offered him.

The blast went straight to his head. "Whoa, where'd you get this?"

"I have my sources. You like it?"

"Maybe," he replied. "Come 'ere. Let me help you with that blouse."

She slid over on the couch. "Be my guest." She smiled seductively.

Trust ran his hands over her cool flesh. She sighed.

"You know what I always wanted to do?" she asked.

"Hmmm," he buried his face between her breasts.

"Make love under the stars."

He leaned back, looked her in the eyes and chuckled. "Oh, I got me a real romantic on my hands." His head was spinning and he felt like superman. He grabbed her by the wrist and pulled her to her feet. "I'm a man that always likes to please the ladies." He led her out to the balcony. She giggled.

"It's a beautiful night," she whispered against his throat. She ran her tongue along the beat of the pulse in his neck while she unbuttoned his shirt and unzipped his pants. Her long fingers played teasing games with him until he pulsed and throbbed in her hands. "Just the way I like it," she purred. She eased his pants down over his hips until they pooled around his ankles. She pulled a small packet from her bra, dipped her long nail into the powder, took a hit then brought it to his nose. "Here, take another hit, you'll last all night."

"You definitely come prepared," he said, snorting deeply, and the world burst into myriad patterns of color and light.

"Always." She leaned back ever so slightly and pushed with all her might.

As Trust sailed over the railing and into the cloudless night, he was so high he truly believed he was flying until seconds before he hit the concrete, seventeen stories below in the courtyard.

Quickly, she picked up the glass she'd been drinking from and stuffed it in her purse along with the wig she'd snatched from her head.

She took a long, hard look around. Satisfied that she'd left no traces of her presence, she wiped the doorknob with a handkerchief on her way out.

CHAPTER TWENTY-FOUR

NOT LIKE THIS

An insistent pounding on the front door jerked Nicole out of a restless sleep. She rubbed her tired eyes and sat up. She looked around, at first disoriented as to where she was. She looked beside her and realized that Trust had never come home.

The pounding came again.

"Take it easy. Damn," she shouted. She pulled herself out of bed and stumbled to the front door. "Who?"

"It's Monroe. Come on, Nik, open up."

She made a face, put the latch on the door, and peeked out. "What the hell is it, Monroe? You know what time it is, man?"

"Open up, Nik. We gotta talk."

"Well, Trust ain't here."

"This is about Trust."

A hot flash raced through her. Her heart pounded. Slowly, she released the latch and opened the door. She put on her hard stance, bracing her hands on her hips. "What is it? And it better not be about some woman."

"Trust is dead, Nik."

For an instant her knees weakened. Monroe grabbed her beneath her arms and led her inside and to the couch.

Slowly she sat down as if in a dream. She looked up at him. "What happened?"

"Nobody knows for sure."

"What the hell are you talking about—nobody knows for sure. Somebody gotta know something!"

"What I mean is nobody knows how it happened."

She took two quick breaths. "Tell me."

"He . . . wound up in the courtyard of the apartment building uptown," he said.

"What? What are you saying? He was shot, mugged, what?"

"He fell off the balcony."

Her head spun. She couldn't breathe. "Off the balcony?" The words seemed to come from some distant place.

She sat there, frozen, visualizing Trust's long descent from the balcony. What was he thinking as he fell? Did all the dirt he'd ever done flash before his eyes?

"What are the police saying?" she managed to get out.

"They ain't saying much and don't seem to really care, ya know? The thing is, I was talking with the boys this morning and we really just want it to all go away. We don't need no police digging in the business. Trust was my man and all, but . . ."

"So what you sayin'? Nobody's gonna try to find out what happened?" Her heart was running a mile a minute.

He shook his head. "Naw. Can't risk it, Nik. You gotta understand our position."

Tears of relief and freedom spilled from her eyes. "So that's the way it's gonna be, huh?" She jumped up. "My man is dead and ya'll just gonna let it ride?"

"That's the way it is. I wanted to come and tell you myself."

"So what's gonna happen with the businesses?"

"I'm running things now." The corner of his mouth lifted momentarily. "You know you always got a spot with us."

She cut her eyes at him. "Very convenient for you, huh, Monroe? You always wanted to be 'the man.'"

His smooth features contracted. "I'll give you a couple of weeks to get yourself straight. Then you're gonna have to book."

She glared at him in disbelief. "You're tellin' me you puttin' me out? This place belongs to Trust."

He shrugged. "I figured since it's my game now, I can run the table any way I want." He glanced around. "I always liked this place." He turned to look at her. "Two weeks."

Nicole watched him leave and flopped back onto the couch. Her mind raced. *Monroe in charge.* Ain't that a bitch? *Trust was dead.* That was what she wanted. Wasn't it? *Of course it was.* All that mattered was that Trust got his payback. Right? *She should be happy.* Right? Then why did she feel so fuckin' shitty?

She looked around. Now she had to figure out what to do with the rest of her life.

CHAPTER TWENTY-FIVE

SO CLOSE

The next few days were a blur for Tess. She moved from morning to night in a daze. The weight of guilt was so heavy at times that she could barely catch her breath.

When she walked into the District Attorney's office, it took all of her wits not to break down and confess what she believed to have taken place. But the cold hard truth was; she had no way of knowing if, in fact, her sister's murder was an act of revenge from her enemies, or the result of her pact with Kim and Nikki. That's what she was there to find out. She needed to know how much Avery know. She understood the risk she was taking by putting herself out in the open, but she had no choice.

"Ms. McDonald, District Attorney Avery was saying, "you have our deepest sympathies."

"Thank you," she murmured.

"I wasn't even aware that Tracy had a sister." His gaze jabbed into her.

"We really haven't been close over the years."

"I see. Well, I'm glad you called us. I know this may

sound . . . insensitive . . . but what proof do you have that you are her sister?"

She'd come prepared. She reached in her purse and produced her birth certificate and that of her sister Tracy. She handed them to Avery.

He looked them over and handed them back. "There is a resemblance. Fraternal?"

Tess nodded.

"Well, the lab has been all over her office, so you are free to . . . take any personal items."

"Thank you," she murmured. "Is there any information on who did this to my sister?" She sniffed.

"We're following up on all the leads, I assure you. We have every reason to believe that it was a hit."

Tess flinched and lowered her head.

"I'm sorry. I didn't mean to be so blunt."

She raised her hand. "It's all right. Tracy always said that threats were a part of the job . . . I just never imagined . . ." Her voice broke.

"None of us did." He pulled a tissue from the box on his desk and handed it to her.

"Thank you." She dabbed at her eyes and stood. "I'd like to get this over with, if you don't mind."

Avery got up as well. "Of course. I'll take you to her office."

They walked out together, passing rows of sympathetic and curious looks.

"I want you to know that all of the arrangements and all expenses are being taken care of. And if there is anything this office can do for you, don't hesitate to ask." He opened the door of Tracy's office.

She turned to him. "Thank you, Mr. Powell."

"It's the least we could do. We all cared for your sister. Just stop at the front desk on your way out so that the secretary can lock up."

Tess nodded. "I will."

Avery tried to smile, turned, and walked away.

Slowly, Tess closed the door, then took a long look around. She needed to assure herself that the D.A.'s office didn't know anything—and they didn't seem to. For a moment, she felt better, a step closer to regaining her life and maintaining her freedom.

She must stay focused in order to get through this, she thought, as she moved through Tracy's office, looking at the degrees and articles framed and mounted on the wall. She took them down and put them in a box on the desk.

She could not risk getting sidetracked, not thinking through every step. The three of them were all intricately linked together. If one stumbled, they all fell.

Tess closed up the box, took a final look around, and walked out.

As she walked down the corridor toward the elevator bank, the sound of rapid-fire commands caught her attention. Her steps slowed.

"I want results. *I mean it!*"

Tess stopped cold. She turned toward the open doorway. Avery glanced up absently, mouthed "good-bye" then resumed his conversation.

A cold sweat began to cover her body. She glanced around quickly as she jabbed the "down" button.

It was the same voice. *The same voice.* Damn, damn, damn.

CHAPTER TWENTY-SIX

WHEN IT'S YOUR TIME

Troy's hands shook ever so slightly as he slowly hung up the phone. A thin line of sweat dribbled down the side of his face and into his right ear. He loosened his tie.

Everything was closing in on him.

"Mr. Benning . . ."

His head snapped up to see his secretary, Michelle, standing in the doorway.

"They're waiting for you in the conference room."

Troy swallowed. "I'll, uh, be right there." He snatched his handkerchief from his jacket pocket and mopped his forehead.

"Are you all right, Mr. Benning?"

He forced a smile. "I'm fine." He stood and adjusted his jacket. "Can you get me the Prescott file?"

"It's right on your desk." She pointed to the red folder.

Troy attempted to shrug it off. He shook his head and chuckled. "Not enough caffeine today. I must still be asleep." He patted the folder, then walked toward the door, stopped and turned. "I'll be leaving for the day after my meeting. Taking a long weekend. If, uh, anything should come up that needs my attention you can reach me on my cell. I'll be at the cabin."

Michelle nodded. "No problem."

Troy walked out.

"Have a good weekend," she called out.

He raised his hand in acknowledgement and kept going.

Troy murmured his apologies for being late and took a seat at the end of the table. He took a quick glance at his always-polished wife at the head of the table and realized just how much he loathed her, almost as much as he was addicted to her. He loathed her success, her intelligence, the way everyone bowed to her, but most of all he loathed the power that she had over him. For years, she'd had him by the nose hairs. He'd been blinded by lust and the good life that her money afforded him. And she used it against him, never allowing him to truly be an active, effective member of the company.

His title, Vice President and CFO, was window dressing. He knew it and so did everyone else. He'd overheard the snide re-marks made about him. Everyone thought he was no more than a pretty face without a useful thought in his head.

"Where do we stand with the promotion of the new linen line, Troy? Do you have the updated figures?"

The sound of his name effectively snapped him out of his twisting thoughts. His gaze darted around the table. All eyes were on him. He shifted in his seat. It took a moment for the question to penetrate.

"I'm working with the final numbers." He cleared his throat. "Everything is coming together."

Kimberly pursed her lips before speaking again. "Can you update us on the progress of the magazine campaign?"

A pin could be heard dropping on the carpet.

"I'll have Michelle put the report on your desk."

Kimberly looked at him for a long moment while several other staff members glanced away.

Bitch. She'd do anything to make him look like a fool, an idiot, in front of everyone. She deserved what was coming to her, and then he would finally get out from under her in more ways than one.

Kimberly cleared her throat and moved on to the next agenda item.

Troy clamped his hands together so tightly his knuckles turned red as Kimberly's even-toned New-England-bred voice grated on his last nerve. He was going to have her where he wanted her or by God he'd kill her himself.

Troy returned to his office, took his trench coat from the closet, and his leather briefcase, with his initials engraved in gold, from beneath his desk.

He started for the door. Kim was standing there.

Troy halted in midstep.

"Half-day?" she said, her sarcasm as thick as the tension in the air.

Troy gritted his teeth. "I have business to tend to, if you don't mind."

Kimberly stepped into the office and closed the door behind her.

"We need to talk, Troy."

"About what this time? Is seduction part of your repertoire again, today?"

She blanched and lifted her chin. "I'm sure you enjoyed it as much as I did." She folded her arms.

"Nice try, Kim. You are still quite incredible, but it hasn't changed my mind. Sign the papers, no contest, and we can move on. If the documents are not signed by Monday, I go to the media."

"Why are you doing this?"

For an instant he was taken aback. Was there a note of pleading in her voice? He almost laughed.

"You know why."

She crossed the room, forcing him to turn around.

"Is it really because of Stephanie?"

"Why else?"

"You're willing to destroy two people's lives and mine just to get back at me?"

"You don't get it, do you?"

"No. Tell me."

"You're too above it all to see what goes on in the world of us mere mortals."

"Don't be cryptic, Troy."

"I know why you married me. To be your beard—your cover—to keep reporters at bay. You never had any intention of letting me ever run anything in the house that Kimberly Sheppard built. Day in and out, I'm humiliated, insulted by the staff, talked about. You really think everyone doesn't know that my position is worth no more than the paper it's written on? That you hold the purse strings and you have them knotted around my neck?"

He paced in front of her. "Did it ever occur to you how that makes me feel? What it does to me as a man? When we married, I had dreams. So much hope for us. I thought we could be a team, really build something together. But that was never *your* plan." He half-smiled. "Was it?"

A momentary sensation of guilty truth pricked her conscience, but quickly passed. "Maybe if you'd done something, anything, with the opportunities that were placed in your lap, handed to you on a silver platter, we wouldn't be having this conversation! When was the last time you made *any* contribution to this company, Troy—finished a project, came up with a coherent idea? If you're not in your favorite bar getting drunk you're in some woman's bed."

His nostrils flared. "Maybe if you were a real woman I'd come home at night." He flashed a nasty grin. "By the way, do you play the man or the woman?"

Kimberly curled her fingers into a fist to keep from wrapping her hands around his throat. "You don't have to do this."

"Oh, yes, I do." He stepped up to her until he was no more than a breath away. "Because you need to know what it feels like to have what's most important to you taken from you. You took my manhood and crushed it beneath your imported high heels." He shoved her out of the way. "Now it's my turn. Sign the papers. I'm not offering options." He opened the door. "Oh, and for the record, the sex was great, but not that great." He walked out.

Kimberly's breath came out in short rapid bursts. She slowly rounded the desk and sat down in Troy's chair. She stared at the open door. She'd hoped there could have been some kind of compromise—a payoff—something.

She lifted her chin and angled her head to the side. He left her no choice. She would not lose, especially to a waste of oxygen like Troy.

Kimberly pushed up from the seat. The only questions that remained were: what would be Troy's demise and how soon.

Troy drove off in his black Mercedes Coupe and headed into midtown Manhattan through a light drizzle. What he needed at the moment was a drink and some time to clear his head. The remnants of that earlier phone call still had him on edge.

When he arrived at his usual spot, it was relatively empty for a Wednesday night, which was fine with him. He greeted the bartender and took his usual seat in the back. Moments later, the waitress arrived with his standard drink, brandy straight up.

"Keep them coming," he said, bringing the glass to his lips.

"Sure thing, Mr. Benning."

Troy gave her his on-camera smile, patted her behind, and took a long swallow of his drink.

By his third drink, he'd successfully sunk deeper into the abyss of his dark, dismal thoughts, but the liquor was making it all bearable.

"Mind if I sit down?"

Troy forced himself to look up. *Not bad.*

"It's a free country," he said, and pulled out a chair next to him.

"Thanks. I hate drinking alone. Men tend to think you're looking for more than a drink, if you know what I mean."

"Go figure." He chuckled.

She put her purse and drink on the table.

She raised her glass. "To better days."

He looked at her through cloudy eyes. *She was hot. Dark hair, great body.* He didn't generally fool around with her kind but . . . tonight, to hell with ethics. "What brings you here, pretty lady?"

She shrugged slightly.

"I needed to unwind, get my head together."

"I know what you mean."

She grinned and moved a little closer. "Handsome man like you should be trouble-free."

He signaled the waitress and requested refills.

"If I play my cards right, I will be."

"I'm a good listener," she said, sipping her rum and Coke.

"Long, ugly story."

"I have time, if you do."

He glanced at her from the corner of his eyes. When was the last time anyone listened to him or wanted to? Besides, he'd never see her again, anyway.

Halfway through his fourth drink he told her what he'd been doing for the past three years: falsifying company documents, funneling the profits from the company into his pockets, and making side deals. "Let's just say that I'm in debt way over my head and the clock is ready to strike midnight. Folks want their money."

Her brow arched. "And you don't have it." It wasn't a question.

He shook his head, tossed his drink down his throat, and signaled for another. "I'm not using my stash. That's for a rainy day."

"Any plans to get it?"

"Yeah, but my lovely wife won't give it to me. So she left me no choice. I had to dig up some dirt on her—use it against her, ya know." He chuckled. "Damn, was she surprised. You shoulda seen the look on her face."

"What did you dig up?"

He managed to get his eyes to focus. Through the thin haze of alcohol, he managed to hold a few things close to his chest. He lowered his voice. "That she's not the lady everyone thinks she is." He snickered at his private joke.

She shook her head and sipped her drink. "So what did you do with all the money?"

The corner of his mouth flickered. "Spent it, lost it, gambled some away."

"Oh. Maybe you could get a bank loan or something."

He chuckled. "I have no collateral. Every stinkin' thing is in that bitch's name!"

"Maybe if you tell her what's going on she would—"

"Never," he ground out. "She wouldn't piss on me if I was on fire and the last soul on earth."

"It can't be that bad."

"Listen, hon, you seem like a real nice girl. But you don't know shit," he slurred. The image in front of him swayed gently to the right, then the left.

He pulled in a deep breath and slowly stood. He took his wallet out of his pants pocket, plucked a hundred-dollar bill from it, and tossed it on the table. "You take care . . ."

She watched him leave. *Good-bye, Mr. Benning.* She pock-
eted the hundred-dollar bill, went to the ladies room and out
the back window.

Troy was drenched by the time he reached his car, a block away
from the bar. It took him several tries to get the key in the ignition. He started to laugh. He laughed so long and hard tears
streamed down his face. Finally, he got the car started and eased
out onto the slick roads.

The windshield wipers were hypnotic as he fought to stay
on his side of the white highway line. He turned up the volume
on the radio and opened the window. Rain splattered him in the
face.

Maybe he should have asked what's-her-name to join him at
the cabin, he thought. Tonight was certainly a night to have a
warm body lying next to you. At this point he'd even settle for
Kim. He started to laugh. How desperate was that?

He stepped on the gas and swerved around a slow-moving
van. She deserved what was coming to her. So what if he'd
stolen from her stupid company? She'd stolen from him, too.

The speedometer rose to seventy.

He could have done great things. But she wouldn't let him.
So he would ruin her life—just like she'd ruined his—and her
little girlfriend, too.

He began to laugh, long and hard. The road ahead became
a blur, replaced by images of Kim pleading with him not to take
her precious little company, not to hurt her precious little
Stephanie.

Suddenly an eighteen-wheel tractor-trailer loomed in front

of him. He tried to swerve out of the way, even as the blaring fog horn of the truck blasted through the night and his clouded brain in concert with the squeal of brakes against the wet road. The car wouldn't obey—just like that damned Kim!

Frantically, he spun the wheel in a complete revolution. The truck whizzed by him so close that the car shook in its frame as the railing and eternity sped toward him.

Troy hit the brakes again . . . again . . . even as he screamed for mercy and forgiveness.

The car, boosted by fuel, power, rage, and free will hurled itself and its passenger over the guardrail, the copse of trees, and down the hundred-foot embankment.

Kim couldn't get the sound of bells out of her head. She turned on her right side, then her left. Finally, she realized it wasn't a dream at all.

Struggling with her eye mask, she slowly sat up in bed.

There it was again. The front doorbell. She glanced at the bedside clock. 4 A.M.

"Who in the . . ." She tossed her legs over the side of the bed, snatched up her robe, and left the bedroom. "Damn you, Troy," she muttered as she went down the stairs. "If you're drunk again . . . Oh, damnit!" She'd slammed her foot into one of the wooden railings on the staircase, and would have tumbled down the rest of the flight if she didn't have the presence of mind to grab the banister. "I will kill you myself!"

She snatched open the door, ready to launch into him, but was stopped cold by the sheriff and a deputy.

"Mrs. Benning?"

"Yes?" She pulled her robe tightly around her. She must look a fright. She brushed her hair away from her face and glanced curiously from one to the other.

"Does your husband drive a black Mercedes Benz?"

"Yes. What is this about?"

"We have some bad news, ma'am."

Every morning news show and every reputable paper was filled with the gory details of the untimely death of Troy Benning, husband of domestic maven, Kimberly Sheppard-Benning. Kimberly had all of the papers spread across her bed. She'd combed the classifieds, looking for the code "Position filled. More opportunities available," as they'd discussed at the hotel. She found nothing. It was just as well. Troy was dead. That's all that mattered, didn't it? She pressed her fist to her mouth to keep from screaming.

The phone wouldn't stop ringing. Reporters were camped out in her front yard.

"Can I get you anything, Mrs. Benning?" Phyllis asked, peeking her head in the door.

Kim jumped at the sound of her housekeeper's voice. "No. Thank you." She slid further down beneath the sheets and mounds of pillows.

"Those reporters are still out there. And your lawyer said he's on his way over."

Kimberly's heart knocked in her chest. She sat up. "Didn't you tell him I wasn't seeing anyone?"

"Yes, ma'am. I told him that you were resting. But he insisted that it was urgent."

She tugged in a breath. "Fine. Let me know when he arrives."

Once Phyllis was out of the room, Kim pulled herself out of the bed, made herself take a shower and get dressed.

From the moment she got the news, she'd vacillated between fear and exhilaration. Fear—that Troy's death, though tragic, would somehow be traced back to her, Tess, and Nikki. Exhilaration—because with Troy out of the way, her business would be saved and her relationship with Stephanie would remain secret.

Still, there was a part of her that beat back the feelings of loss. Ten years of marriage, though troubled, was over; a life she'd shared with someone had ended.

There had been something between her and Troy. She even believed that Troy would be the one to keep her hidden desires at bay. For a while, he did. But it turned ugly between them over the years, growing worse with the passage of each day.

Unfortunately, in the world of business, as in life, the first law of man is survival of the fittest. As she stood in front of the mirror brushing her hair, she wondered which one of them did it and how they'd managed.

Kimberly stared at her reflection. It was best that she didn't know.

CHAPTER TWENTY-SEVEN

THE FACTS OF THE MATTER

"How are you, Kim?" her attorney asked.

She brought a white handkerchief to her eyes. "As well as can be expected, John."

He looked around to ensure that no one was in the vicinity. He lowered his voice. "You, uh, didn't have anything to do with . . ."

Her blue eyes widened in watery disbelief. "I can't believe you asked me something like that."

He cleared his throat. "You have to admit, the timing is . . . convenient. You were in my office only a few weeks ago saying you wanted him dead," he whispered, his expression tense.

She waved him off. "I was upset. But that doesn't mean that I would kill my own husband. I wanted what was mine. That's what I have a lawyer for. And quite frankly, John, I'm insulted that you would even think it and worse, say it."

"I'm sorry. It's just . . . I was out of line."

"Yes, you were."

"Is there anything you need me to do?"

"No, the service is scheduled for the day after tomorrow." Her eyes filled. "I can't believe he's gone," she cried, her voice breaking with emotion. She lowered her head.

John came to sit beside her. He put his arm around her shoulder. "I'm here for you, Kim. Whatever you need."

"Thank you," she whimpered. "I really appreciate it."

Slowly he eased his arm away. "I'll let you get some rest."

"Are those reporters still outside?"

"A few stragglers."

"He was drunk the M.E. said," she blurted out.

John nodded his head.

"Nothing left of the car and not much left of . . ." She buried her face in her handkerchief.

"I know this sounds naïve but try not to think about it. You'll make yourself ill."

"I know, I know." She looked up at him. "Thanks for stopping by, John."

"Of course. I'll see you at the service."

She watched him walk out and twisted her mouth in contemplation. Soon this would all be over. Troy would be six feet under and she could move on with her life.

She wondered how Tess was doing now that her sister was out of the way and the investigation seemed to have come to a halt. The newspapers and broadcasts provided what little news they had on a daily basis . . . *no leads*. She didn't expect to see any news about Nicole's little problem. After all he was a common criminal.

She lifted her chin in triumph. Each of their ugly wishes had come true.

———

Nicole packed up the last of her belongings that she'd brought with her to Trust's apartment. She couldn't believe that after all she'd been through and done for the crew that Monroe would dare kick her to the curb. It was a miracle he "allowed" her to attend Trust's funeral services.

At least she could go home. Maybe she'd convince the doc to take her back at the office—even part time. She'd get her life together and maybe Ricky would finally let her spend some of the money she'd been saving and fix up the apartment, buy some new furniture and things he needed. She'd buy a car and help her sister get one, too, when she graduated from high school. Maybe they'd even find a better apartment in a nice neighborhood. She smiled at the possibilities. She'd find a way to take care of her family. Finally.

When she arrived at the apartment she'd lived in most of her life, she found it empty. Confused, she walked inside and went from room to room. All of them were empty. What she was see-ing didn't make sense. Of course she thought the worst. Some-thing had happened to Ricky and Julia. It was some kind of payback. *Dios mio.*

She ran downstairs and banged on the landlord's door.

When he opened it, his lecherous smile turned her stomach. "Well, *chica*. What can I do for you?"

"What happened upstairs? Where are my brother and sis-ter?" She planted her hands on her hips, ready to fight.

He moved the stinking cigar from one side of his mouth to

the other and grinned at her with brown teeth. "I guess they didn't tell you that they were moving, huh, *chica*."

She frowned. "What the fuck are you talking about?"

"Is that any way for such a pretty girl to talk?"

"Where are they, Louie?"

"Gone. Moved out two days ago." He chewed on the cigar.

Her heart thumped. "What?"

"Moved out, gone vamoose."

"I don't believe you."

He shrugged. "Don't." Then he grinned. "I could give you a good deal on the apartment. You take care of me and I could see about letting you live rent free."

"Go to hell." She spun around and ran back upstairs, determined to find some clue, some bit of information to tell her where her siblings had gone.

She searched the empty closets, behind doors, the windowsills. Nothing. With each passing moment the rotten reality of what happened began to settle in her belly like uncooked meat left out in the sun.

Disbelief then acceptance left her weak. They'd gone. They'd left her behind to move on with life—without her.

Nicole wasn't sure how long she sat in the middle of the empty room. When she looked up, it was dark outside and the smell of onions, beans, and chicken seeped through the walls.

She looked around in bewilderment. What had it all been for? Now she had nothing. No fabulous life, no family. Nothing.

Bitter tears slid down her cheeks. She cried until exhaustion overtook her and she fell asleep in a fetal position on the floor.

———

Tess never fully understood her sister's importance or how much she was cared about until the day of her funeral. Everyone had something good to say about her. That was generally the case at most funerals. No one wanted to be caught saying something ill of the dead.

But if there was ever a reason for her to leave town and start over, it was now. Until the murder, no one really knew about her and she wanted to keep it that way. During and following the service, she'd tried to remain as inconspicuous as possible but Avery Powell made sure that he introduced her to every soul he could summon to his side, and he never left hers. Her growing trepidations about Avery and fear for her freedom only intensified in his presence. He'd stuck so close that by the time she got back to her apartment, she swore she could smell his cologne on her clothes.

She wondered how many of her former clients may have recognized her and were squirming in their seats when they saw her in the newspapers standing next to the District Attorney. Hopefully, she'd used the disguise of grief to full advantage, and unless they could identify her from the lips down, they should be able to sleep with confidence at night. She was safe now, and so were the women who worked for her and her clients. *A sacrifice of one for the good of the many.* Viewing it from that perspective was the only way she could look at her reflection after what she'd set in motion.

Stripping, she walked from one room of her apartment to the next, contemplating her future. With all the money she'd stashed away she could live comfortably for the rest of her life anywhere in the world. Although her business was dismantled, she knew she would begin again. There were plenty of women who craved excitement, entertainment, the opportunity to meet important men and make an incredible amount of money—simply by being a woman.

Tess stood naked in front of the bathroom mirror. In a few more years, without a little help, she knew time, age and use would begin to catch up with her. New York was a heartless city in which to grow old, plus the incentive of needing to get away from the people who now knew her relationship with Tracy was even more reason to escape as quickly as possible.

Day after tomorrow was Troy Benning's funeral. *The last of the three.* After that she would make her plans to leave. Someplace warm, she thought. Yes, someplace sunny and warm.

CHAPTER TWENTY-EIGHT

RETRIBUTION

The Amtrak train pulled into the 30th Street, Philadelphia station.

Nicole picked up her bag and stepped off into the bustling throng of passengers. Today was her new beginning—alone. It had taken her days to realize that her sister and brother were not coming back. She'd slept on the floor of the apartment, praying that when she awoke, she would inhale the smells of her brother fixing breakfast and the sounds of her sister getting ready for school. It never happened.

She spent the next few days combing the streets, asking all the shopkeepers and neighbors if anyone had seen them. The only iota of hope she held was a comment her brother made years earlier, that if he had a chance he would leave New York and move to Philadelphia. There was a lot of building and renovation going on in Philadelphia and more opportunity for him, he'd said.

So here she was, in a strange city, with nothing but a suitcase filled with money and hope in her pocket.

———

Kimberly arrived early to her office on Monday morning. It was her first day back since . . . She felt moderately refreshed after her weekend in Baltimore and her brief meeting with Nicole and Tess on the train. No matter what she might have thought of either of them, they were bound together by their deadly secret for all eternity. Their last and final meeting served as confirmation and also a mirror, the enormity of what had transpired reflected in each of their eyes. She'd never see them again. In a way it made her sad, knowing that there was no one on earth with whom she shared something so terribly intimate, not even Stephanie.

She'd stayed at a resort near the Baltimore Harbor. The time away from the pressure of the job, the hounding of reporters, and the somber feel in her home, did her good. It was the first time in weeks that she'd slept without having nightmares about what happened—what they'd conspired to do. The constant fear of discovery was never more than a breath away. For each hour that ticked by on the clock, the closer she felt toward total freedom.

Walking through the halls of her offices was surreal. She passed by what had been Troy's office and a sharp, stabbing pain pierced her stomach. For a moment, her throat tightened in a flash of regret, but just as quickly the sensation left her.

Kimberly pulled in a deep, cleansing breath and opened her office door. Today would mark a new beginning.

As the day progressed, her staff slowly shifted from tentative and hushed in her presence to energized and chatty, bringing her up to date on current projects and the latest dramas in their personal lives. This was what she needed.

Her intercom halted her conversation with her home products designer. "One minute," Cynthia," she said. She went over to her desk and picked up the phone. "Yes?"

"Mrs. Benning, Phillip Sachter the Senior Accountant is on the phone."

"Put him through." She blew out a breath of annoyance. Phillip was one of the most boring individuals on the face of the earth. His entire life revolved around numbers. Any subject beyond that and he turned into an amoeba.

"Hello, Phillip. What can I do for you?"

"We have a major problem, Mrs. Benning. I need to speak with you right away."

"What is it about?"

"I'd rather discuss this with you in person. I can come to your office now."

Kimberly frowned, the sound of urgency in his voice sent a sense of unease through her. "Fine." She hung up. "Cynthia, I'm sorry. We're going to have to get back together later. Something has come up." She forced a smile.

Cynthia closed up the portfolios that were spread out on the rectangular conference table. "No problem. This will keep. Give me a call when you have some time."

Kimberly nodded.

Pensive, she paced in front of her desk until a short sharp knock slowed then halted her steps.

"Come in."

"Mr. Schater is here to see you," her assistant announced.

"Come in, Phillip."

Pale and gaunt, Phillip entered the office with his ever-ready bulging satchel tucked beneath his right arm. He closed the door behind him.

"Have a seat," she said, indicating a chair at the table.

"Thank you," he murmured. He opened his briefcase and spread what looked like a ton of papers and folders on the table. He cleared his throat and looked at his boss through watery eyes, magnified a hundred times through thick, black-framed glasses. He always reminded her of a cartoon character.

"What is this about?"

"Mrs. Benning. Uh, since, Mr. Benning's uh, passing, I have been going over the books. And . . ."

"Get to the point, Phillip."

"You're nearly bankrupt, Mrs. Benning," he blurted out. He pushed his glasses farther up on his pointed nose.

For an instant she couldn't make sense of what he was saying. "What in the world are you talking about?"

"It appears that Mr. Benning had been using company funds and profits for . . . personal use from each of the divisions."

Kimberly blinked rapidly and with shaky fingers she tucked her hair behind her ears. Slowly she sat down. "That's not possible," she sputtered.

"It's very possible. He had access, Mrs. Benning." He flipped open a folder. "I went over everything with a fine tooth comb. The money is there in theory but not reality. It's practically gone."

Kimberly's heart raced so rapidly she could barely breathe.

"It gets worse."

Her blue eyes snapped in his direction.

"Your name is on the loan notes along with his to casinos in Atlantic City, Vegas, and Arizona."

"What?"

Slowly he bobbed his small head, his dark, stringy hair dipping across his forehead.

"I haven't signed any loan notes!"

He pulled a sheaf of papers from the folder and slid them across the desk. "They are in excess of twenty million dollars. Apparently this has been going on for quite some time."

The room grew uncomfortably warm. The numbers danced in front of her face. She pressed her palms flat down on the table. "What do we do?" Each word strained to come out.

"You're going to have to close several of the divisions. You will have to inform your board of directors, immediately. There's not enough cash flow to pay the stockholders their dividends this quarter. The stocks will plummet. And you will have to find a way to pay back these loans."

"I . . ." She stood. "How could you not have known?"

"I can only work with what I'm given, Mrs. Benning. And with Mr. Benning being Vice President and CFO, I went to him for all the financial documents." He lowered his head for a moment then looked across at her. "It's possible that there could be a federal investigation, Mrs. Benning." He paused. "I'm sorry."

Kimberly frowned, looking at him as if he'd suddenly appeared. She tried to focus, but everything seemed hazy and slightly out of reach.

"Thank you, Phillip," she said, her voice sounding as if it came from some distant place. "You can go now."

"Mrs. Benning, I really think . . ."

"You can go now, Mr. Sachter," she said with more force. Her eyes burned into his.

He gathered up his papers and stuffed them back into his bag. "We need to work something out, Mrs. Benning, and quickly." He picked up his bag and left.

For several interminable minutes, Kimberly sat motionless. Everything she'd worked for, sacrificed for, was gone—anyway. She started to laugh and laugh. She couldn't stop. Tears rolled down her cheeks. It was all for nothing.

If there was any way she could have Troy murdered again and again, she would. No wonder he was so hellbent on getting her to sign quickly. It was the only way he could cover his tracks, and he'd probably take whatever was left to pay off his debts before he ran the company completely into the ground. But what would happen to his mealticket then? Did he really hate her so much that he was willing to lose everything? *Or maybe all that money wasn't really gone at all.* Troy may have been vindictive, but he was not an idiot. He was a greedy bastard. Knowing him, he had an exit plan. Damn you, Troy.

Drawing on the inner strength that had sustained her for years, she pushed up from the table and went to her desk. She pressed the button for her assistant.

"Yes, Mrs. Benning?"

"Marie, I want you to get all of the department heads together for an emergency meeting in one hour. There's something I need to tell them."

"Right away."

She released the intercom and turned to look out the window at life on the street below.

More than a decade earlier, she'd started with no more than a dream and five thousand dollars in savings. She'd come from basically nothing, a small-town girl from a rural spot in Maine whose biggest thrill was going to the "city" to visit the library. Her dad was a factory worker and her mom did day-work for the wealthy folks in town. Both of them worked long hours, often leaving her alone with "Uncle Joe." She was the first one to go to college in her entire family and she swore when she got her first degree that she was never going back to that life. She was going to remake herself, build a world like she'd only seen in magazines and on television. She'd done it. And now . . . Somehow she would find a way to regroup, clean up the mess that Troy left behind and begin again. No matter what it took.

Kimberly thought of Nicole and Tess and what would ultimately become of *their* lives. Retribution makes strange bedfellows.

She turned away from the window and prepared to face her staff.

Avery Powell sat in a back booth in a small diner just off West Third Street. It was out of the way and inconspicuous. He sipped on his second cup of coffee and stared at the headline of the *Daily News*. His office was under federal investigation for allegations of fraud and tampering with evidence. And it all pointed back to Tracy Alexander. Whatever hopes he had for reelection and then higher office would be submerged in a cloud of scandal for years to come.

He glanced up as a shadow appeared above him. "Have a seat."

"Things are not looking good in the neighborhood."

Avery averted his gaze. "I'll probably have to resign before this whole ugly mess is over."

"I'm sorry."

"Are you? Seems to me you're part of the problem."

"I'm a free agent, Avery. I go where the job takes me. What happens behind *your* closed doors has nothing to do with me. You hired me to do a job."

"And you came up empty. Or so you say." He looked at him hard. "Where is she, Vincent?"

"She gave me the slip."

"Bullshit. In all the years I've known you, you've always found your man—or woman."

Vincent chuckled. "Can I be frank?"

"Aren't you always?"

He crossed his arms on the table and leaned forward. "I think that your issues are much bigger than finding some woman who makes her living "entertaining" men. Don't you?"

Avery brought the coffee cup to his lips and finished it off. "I suppose you're right. Guess that's my payback for trying to get an inside track on the Madam X case. I had a gut feeling in the beginning that Tracy was holding back information on the case." He looked directly at Vincent. "That's why I brought you in." He toyed with his empty cup. "Guess you both screwed me." He slowly shook his head. "But I never imagined that Tracy was capable of doing what she's accused of. I knew she was ambitious and I knew she was hoping to have my job one day. But I never thought that she would manufacture evidence, bribe witnesses and who knows what else just to win her cases. If she hadn't been killed, we might have never known what she'd been up to. But when the Attorney General wanted all the data on Madam X and there were no files . . . at least none of value, well all hell broke loose. They're going to dig all the way to China."

"One thing I've learned in this business buddy is that most people are definitely not what they seem."

Avery released a long breath. He looked at Vincent, his friend since childhood. They'd always been as different as night and day. Avery was always trying to do the right thing. Vincent was always just shy of the right side of the law. They'd been covering each other's backs for years in one form or another. But today he had a feeling that he wouldn't see his friend again.

"You fell for her, didn't you?" he asked as the knowledge settled in his gut.

Vincent gave him a quarter of a smile. "I'm no fool, Avery. And let's leave it at that."

Avery slowly stood. Vincent followed.

"Is there anything that I can do?" Vincent asked.

"I'll be fine." He stuck out his hand.

Vincent came around the table and wrapped him in a bear hug. "Take it easy, man." He turned to walk out. Avery's comment stopped him.

"Oh, whenever you see her again, let her know we have Tracy's killer in custody."

CHAPTER TWENTY-NINE
GETTING HERS

Tess lay stretched out on a beach chair next to the pool, clad in a scanty burnt orange bikini. A wide-brimmed straw hat with a burnt orange bandana obscured her features.

Aruba was an exquisite place, she mused as she sipped on her tropical drink, topped with a tiny pink paper umbrella and a cherry. She adjusted her dark glasses and closed her eyes.

More than two months had passed since she'd stepped off the train in Washington. She spent a week there, haunting the shops, taking tours and simply letting her mind unwind after months of tension and anxiety.

When she was certain that her funds were securely transferred, she hopped a plane and began her new life in the Caribbean.

"Tess."

She tipped up the brim of her hat and peeked up over the rim of her sunglasses. She smiled.

"I've arranged to have the ladies meet us in your suite at seven," Charrie said.

As soon as Tess was settled in her new home she'd called the states and tracked down Charrie. They'd built her New York business together and she couldn't think of anyone else to help her start anew.

Charrie took the lounge chair next to Tess. "Never thought I'd be back in the game again," she said, signaling one of the waitresses for a fresh drink.

"For a while, neither did I." She hadn't told Charrie about what happened back in New York. Maybe she would one day. "Are you all set to go to the airport?"

"Yes. I have it all worked out. The flights are an hour apart."

Tess reached for her pack of Newports. "I'll have a nice spread ready when you get back. To celebrate."

"Wonderful," Charrie murmured and took a sip of her wine spritzer, her signature drink. "It'll be great to be back in business again, Tess."

"It certainly will."

As promised, Tess had a spread fit for a delegation of royalty. Delicacies from the island graced three serving tables; fish, fowl, steamed vegetables, salads, rice, and baby potatoes. Two tables held desserts, enough to send anyone into diabetic shock. The heavenly aroma filled the air lifted by the light sea breeze blowing in off the terrace. She'd even hired a local combo that was playing calypso in the background.

"This is fabulous, Tess," a gorgeous Ethiopian woman murmured over the rim of her champagne glass.

"It's only the beginning, Amina." Tess gently patted her shoulder. "Only the beginning."

Tess looked around. She'd successfully recruited six new women, covering as many nationalities, all of them beautiful, intelligent, and willing. Several of her New York ladies had also accepted her offer and were in attendance as well. Tonight was to solidify and celebrate their business arrangement.

She crossed the white-washed floor, her ankle length broomstick skirt flowing around her as she stepped out to the terrace. On the beach below she watched several couples laughing, hugging, and planning for the night ahead. For a moment, a pang of regret beat against her chest. A foolish part of her had hoped that she would be looking forward to a life with Vincent. Girlish dreams.

"Tess. Tess."

She turned to the sound of Charrie's voice and a slow, deliberate smile spread across her mouth. Her long legs took her across the open space in quick, smooth strides.

"Nicole. Kim. So glad you two still read the classifieds." She reached out and clasped their hands in each of hers.

"An invitation to Aruba. How could a girl resist?" Nicole quipped.

Kimberly took in the space in a slow sweeping glance. "No one can ever say you don't have style, Tess."

Tess laughed.

"I could get used to this," Nicole said. "Real easy." She grinned.

"I hope you both can," Tess said. "Success is nothing without someone to share it with." She winked.

"*Lady Sings the Blues*," Nicole said, laughing.

Tess held their hands. "Let me introduce you to everyone."

After introductions, Tess clapped her hands and got everyone's attention.

"Ladies, I want to welcome you all. The life you are stepping into will open new worlds for you, new opportunities, and provide you with a great deal of money."

The women laughed.

"So I want you to get to know each other. These will be the women you will come to rely on, depend on."

Tess moved among her guests while she spoke. "What our clients look for, each of you possess: intelligence, beauty, sensuality and most of all discretion. This is not a business for the loose lips. The only way we can protect ourselves and our clients is to never let what we do or what we know move outside of our circle—ever." She looked at each woman in turn. "The gentlemen will be arriving shortly. Make them feel like kings. Enjoy yourselves and welcome to the family."

Tess went to check with the waiters to make sure that there was enough food. She took time to speak with each of the women and finally she was able to sit and talk with Nicole and Kim.

"I read what happened, Kim," Tess said. "I'm sorry."

"It was certainly a shock. I picked up as many pieces as I could, paid off what I could and filed Chapter 11. The lawyers and the accountants are still trying to track the money that Troy stole. But between their fees and my own legal expenses, I'll need to use whatever they find to pay everyone off. This invitation was a godsend."

"What about Stephanie?" Tess asked.

Kim looked away for a moment. "Let's put it this way, I'll get over it and I'm sure she already has. Being here is about starting over."

"Until I saw the ad in the paper offering a new start, 'not all positions filled,' I wasn't sure what I was going to do in a strange city," Nicole said. "I still have no idea where my sister and brother are. You don't know how many times I looked at the number before I decided to take a chance and call."

"I'm glad you're both here," Tess said, looking from one to the other. "This is not just a job, it's an adventure, using what you already have and know to make it work. I need two strong women like you to help me run things. Charrie and I can't do it alone, not with my plans to expand. What better choices than you both?"

Kim and Nicole shared a look of surprised interest.

There's money to be made ladies, a lot of it."

"Tess, sorry to interrupt. You have a call," Charrie said.

"Who is it?"

"I'm sorry. It was so noisy, I didn't ask."

"Okay. Excuse me." She started for the phone and had a sudden flash of déjà vu. The last time Charrie took a call like that her business came tumbling down. You're just being silly, she thought as she picked up the phone in the foyer.

"Hello?" She covered her free ear with her hand.

"You're a very ingenious woman."

"Who is this?" But even as she asked the question, she knew the answer.

"Nikki . . ."

"Hmmm?" She sipped her rum punch.

"Speaking of ads, did you ever place your ad in the classifieds like we discussed that night in my hotel room?"

For an instant, Nicole's dark eyes flashed. Was she being set up? It was a question that had haunted her for months. Should she lie? She was finally free from the past, she couldn't go back. She wanted to put . . . all that stuff behind her. This was her life now, a life she'd chosen, but the guilt of it all had been eating her alive.

"No. I never did." She looked Kim square in the eye, waiting for one of her nasty comments.

The air stuck in the center of Kim's chest. "Neither did I."

Nicole frowned. "Then how . . . who did you have?"

"What does it matter? It's done. They're all dead and buried."

Nicole grabbed Kim by her bare arms and shook her. "Tell me, please." Her heart was racing at a frightening rate. "I've got to know or I'll go out of my mind."

"Why?"

Her chest heaved. "Because they're all dead and I know I didn't kill anyone."

Kim blinked. Her cheeks slowly grew red. "What? What are you saying?"

"I didn't kill anyone," Nicole hissed, her eyes darting around the room.

Kim felt momentarily weak. "Trust," she said, barely above a whisper. "I had Trust."

Nicole let go of Kim and stumbled backward. The contents of her stomach rose to her throat. "You . . . you pushed him over the balcony?" she asked, her voice taut and high pitched.

Kim swallowed. "I never got a chance to," she said.

"What?" She pressed the heel of her palm to her forehead.

"I didn't kill Trust, Nicole. I thought about it, all the likely ways. I even went so far as to get a supply of cocaine from Stephanie. But I didn't kill him."

Nicole lowered her head a moment, uncertain whether it was relief or contempt that she was feeling. She looked up at Kim. "I had Tess's sister. But I didn't kill her. I swear to you."

"Tess," Kim said from between her teeth. "She did it all. She had to have done it. It was her scheme from the beginning."

"God." Nicole looked around, spotting Tess, still on the phone. "What are we going to do?"

"Nothing." She looked Nicole straight in the eyes. "It's our secret. Always. Tess is giving us a second chance. She did this for us. She deserves a second chance, too. All of us are in this together and we can never tell." Kim insisted. "Aren't we all better off with those bastards out of our lives?"

Nicole nodded numbly and reached for a glass of wine from a passing waiter. Her hand shook. She knew Kim was lying. She never even reacted when she was asked if she'd pushed Trust over the balcony. *She never got a chance to.* Why would that be her answer if she didn't do it? And there was no way for her to know unless she was there. Trust's murder was never even a blip in the papers.

"Just like that night in the hotel was our secret, so is this," Kim was saying. She captured the next waiter and snatched a glass from the tray, bringing it steadily to her lips. They were all fools if they thought she would be stupid enough to place an ad in the paper, no matter how innocuous. Nothing must ever be tied to her and that night.

Kim glanced off toward the horizon and wondered when she

would finally stop seeing Trust's accusing eyes staring up at her as she pushed him over the balcony and he hurtled to his death. One day the visions would end, she was sure of it. She tapped her long nail against her glass before draining it of its contents.

Tess gripped the phone a bit tighter.

"The jig, as they say, is up, Tess." He paused. "I know every-thing. And now you're all back together again like one happy family. Naughty girls."

"I don't know what you're talking about, Vincent."

He laughed. "Of course you do. But that's not why I called."

"Really? Then why did you call?"

"You should have told me you were leaving, Tess. I had all the evidence I needed to bring you down, but I didn't. You ever ask yourself why? And then one day, poof, you vanish, without a word. That hurt, Tess."

"Vincent . . ."

"You can't continue to get away with ruining lives, Tess. I won't let you. Not this time."

"You've got this all wrong, Vincent." *Think, Tess, think.*

"I have all the proof I need. I've been onto you for months. Do you really think our meeting was accidental? I'm good at what I do."

"Where are you? We should talk—face to face." Her eyes darted around the room. Everyone was enjoying themselves.

"In town, in the motel on Laguna Cove."

Her mind raced. "I'll meet you." She swallowed. "Is . . . Avery with you?"

Vincent chuckled. "That's what I like about you, Tess, you're smart. But like I told you in the beginning, I work alone." He paused. "I'll be here, waiting. We have a lot to talk about."

Slowly she hung up the phone. Her expression was resolute, but her heart was heavy. Weaving around her guests, she got upstairs to her bedroom, opened the dresser drawer and withdrew her .38. She stared at the white envelope embossed with the Sheraton Hotel logo. The slip inside was blank and always had been. She'd been the lucky one. But the joke was on her. She'd started this as a drunken lark that had taken on an unspeakable turn, setting off a chain of events that coerced two women into committing cold-blooded murder. She'd wanted to test her powers of persuasion, and she had. She'd forever carry that weight on her shoulders. Now was her chance to balance the scales and put them all back on the same equal footing. She couldn't be sure what and how much Vincent actually knew, but she wasn't taking any chances. She'd slipped once with Vincent when she'd allowed emotions to sneak in. Once was too many. It wouldn't happen again. There was only one way to keep Vincent from ever telling anyone what he knew. She checked the gun clip, stuck the gun in her purse, and returned downstairs.

Nicole and Kimberly were out on the terrace.

"I need to go out for a while," she said, walking in on the end of their conversation.

"Now?" they asked in unison.

"Yes. Charrie can handle this. And she'll know what to do should anything *ever* go wrong." She looked first at Nicole and then Kimberly. "Remember that story I told in the elevator about that guy with the great biceps?"

They nodded, frowning a bit in confusion.

"It's time to end it." Tess gave them a tight but determined smile, turned and walked out.

Slowly, understanding hit them then spread like liquid across fabric. Kimberly and Nicole simultaneously reached for each other's hand. The rev of Tess's car engine could be heard over the pulsing beat of the combo.

As the sound of Tess's car grew faint, Nicole thought back to how easy it had been to rig Troy Benning's Mercedes. The rainy night and a belly full of liquor was icing on the cake. It was even easy to lie about it to his happy widow; one of her better performances if she had to say so herself. As for the ad, if there was one thing she'd learned from that *bastardo*, Trust, it was that a good businessperson didn't need to advertise, clients would find them. She squeezed Kim's hand. They'd all get through this. Tess would make sure of it, and whatever happened would remain secret between the three of them forever.

LETTER TO READERS

Hello All,

Thanks so much for taking a chance on *Getting Hers*. For those of you who have read my previous work, this is a definite departure, but I hope you enjoyed it. For those who may be reading me for the first time, I hope it will not be your last.

Getting Hers is certainly a cautionary tale of secrets, retribution, and wishes gone wild, and creating the characters that would be able to pull off a storyline of "what ifs" was definitely a challenge. Very often in life, we are unaware of the chain of events that one simple act can cause. Tess, Nicole, and Kim set off on a course of no return and soon discover that thinking a dirty deed can be as lethal as actually doing it. They have since learned to be careful what they wish for. Or have they?

And what of Tess? Does she actually kill Vincent? Does she change her mind when she is face-to-face with that reality, or will her sense of duty overshadow her feelings for the man who could destroy her? Hmmm. Sounds like a sequel! Time will tell. I'd love to hear your thoughts. Send me an email at donna199@hotmail.com.

In the meantime, thank you for your support and for coming along for the ride.

Until next time,

Donna

ABOUT THE AUTHOR

Donna Hill's first novel was published in 1990. She currently has thirty-eight titles in print which include twenty-four novels and sixteen short stories. Three of her novels, *Intimate Betrayal*, *A Private Affair*, and *Masquerade*, were adapted for and aired on television. Donna's writings cross genres from romance to general fiction, from erotica to horror to comedy. She has won numerous awards for her body of work and has been recognized for her community service. She conceptualized and edited two award-nominated anthologies, *After the Vows* and *Midnight Clear*. Her novel *Divas Inc.* sparked the launch of the Divas Incorporated Society, a nationwide, not-for-profit organization dedicated to empowering women and girls, and offering grants and scholarships to qualified applicants. A portion of the proceeds from her novel *In My Bedroom* is being donated to Safe Horizons, an organization that offers assistance, resources, and support to women and girls who have been, or are in, abusive situations on a variety of levels (safehorizons.org). Donna currently works as a public relations associate for the Queens Library system. She lives in Brooklyn, New York, with her family. For more information, visit her Web site at http://donnahill.com.